THIS IS A CHICAGO PAPERBACK ORIGINAL OF
JEFF TYLER AND HIS LOAFALONG, THE SECOND
OF A LONG CHAIN OF JEFF TYLER-LOAFALONG
ADVENTURES THAT WE HOPE TO PUBLISH. THE
FIRST BOOK, 'ROOM AT THE BOTTOM'—ASK
YOUR DEALER FOR IT IF HE'S SOLD OUT.

—OR MURDER FOR FREE

by

J. L. POTTER

—OR MURDER FOR FREE

PROLOGUE

The street was quiet as he picked up the newspaper thrown carelessly on the lawn and put his key into the lock of the dingy front door. He'd found the door locked at the end of every shift for months; it was a measure designed at least, to delay intruders, to give if nothing more, momentary warning. And during these past months he'd made his way furtively home, arriving an hour after the others on the block.

Inside the house was steamy and aromatic, its atmosphere heavy with the odors of a house shut up through a long winter, a house not quite due for spring cleaning and airing. Tossing the paper onto the rickety couch, the overcoat, threadbare in spots, but familiar, following it, he picked up the lone letter from the tray on the end table and glanced at the bold hand directing it to Heinrich Strobel. The curves and angles were familiar; his hand shook just a bit as he crumbled it, unopened, then, feeling rage, hurled the missive into a dark corner – one where the old carpet still looked new.

"Allo, Dad." The woman, aging now, showed signs of an earlier beauty, not completely concealed by the extra pounds time and four children had added to her short, slight frame. He seldom thought of her these days as she'd once been; for years she had been 'mother' to him and the brood of growing children that sapped all her time and his money. The greying hair was unkempt and straggling, the cheap cotton dress of gaudy Bemberg-like floral print had its split seams and tears hidden by a still cheaper cotton apron, itself in disrepair.

"Allo, Mother," he acknowledged, tiredly — then — though the acrid odor left no doubt that sauerkraut was simmering on the old range, added, "What's for supper?"

"Bad day?"

"Terrible. They got Tarnowski last night. Tonight, soon, they get me. I am last."

She put a finger to bloodless lips. "The children," she warned. "Do not frighten the children. Was it bad? Tarnowski, I mean?"

"Probably he will die. And his youngest boy, die or live crippled and disfigured. Pray, Annie — pray he will die."

"Supper. Eat. You will feel better, father."

He tried the door, nodded reassured at the sturdiness of the lock and followed his wife into the small pink and yellow kitchen, a kitchen whose walls were stained with the steam of numberless meals, whose floral curtains showed the dulling of years of exposure to the western sun. Already the four children, three girls and one boy, stood behind their chairs in respectful silence. Harry, the oldest boy, smiled a greeting to the man who now was larger, but still master of the family.

"Allo, children," the weary voice greeted softly. "You may seat yourselves now." Still they stood in silence; only when he had slid into his chair did they follow. Annie set a great steaming toureen on the table; The center leaf groaned and settled under the weight, the aroma of the kraut thickened in the air. Vegetables and hot rolls followed, finally, she too pulled back her chair, sat heavily and smiled at the waiting group who took their cue to lower their heads in reverence.

"Lord," the flat voice of the senior man intoned without emotion, "Thank you for the fare you put before us this day. Help us to be deserving of it, to work hard and honestly, and to live in peace. Help us," the voice got harsher, angry, "to value honesty and to survive against those—against those who would rob us of human dignity, who would imprison us in the toils of greed and thievery, who would rob and pilfer and blackmail and kill, and would make us do the same." He was almost raging now, under the weight of his constant fear. "Help us to defeat these oppressors, to thwart their lust for blood and money, to-"

"The children, father," Annie muttered. "The children."

"God help us all, then, Amen."

Pandemonium broke loose as the children, served in turn from the oldest to youngest, tried to intersperse reports on the day's school and play between gulps of food. There was no restraint—all chattered about unrelated adventures, all tried to out-talk, in speed and in volume, the other contenders. All but the boy, normally garrulous, as could be expected of any fifteen year old, who consumed his food in stolid silence, a heavy frown distaining the small talk that raged around him.

"Son," Heinrich inquired finally, "cat got your tongue?"

"The children, father. May I talk to you this evening?"

"We alarmed you then—mother and I. Pay no attention to what we have said. How was school today?"

"Please, after supper."

"Very weak." He returned to parrying the amazing whys of the youngsters—why didn't teachers smile, why wasn't a person called 'long-faced' a conspicuous freak, why did the geography book call the earth an oblate spheroid when father had told them all these years that it was round? Soon it was over. The girls rushed out to enjoy a last few minutes of play in the cool twilight, Annie busied herself in the after-dinner kitchen work as the Heinrichs, Junior and Senior, entered the living room, seated themselves uneasily in upholstered chairs — garish plush monstrosities of the sort purporting to convey a measure of luxury, but failing miserably in their shoddy transparent effort. The silence was brief, but embarrassed. Finally words tumbled out.

"Father, I'm old now. Old enough to know about these things. I won't scare the kids or get excited and rash or anything. Don't you think it's time I started helping you? After all, I get my share in school — their kids get to me there just like they get to you at work."

"Son, a moment. Calm a moment, please."

"But father," he stopped at the sight of an upheld arm, a gesture for silence.

"These things are for men to deal with. What about school, now?"

"I didn't say — "

"You did. What about school, son? You just asked me to confide in you; isn't it right for you to be just as frank as you want me to be?"

"Allright. It's just what you must get all the time. Remember, last week — the cut eye and bruises I wouldn't talk about?"

"They did that?"

"Our teacher says they're right. So do our books on social science. They say you — we — are taking food from their babies and stealing from them."

"What do you think?"

"That they are thieves and murderers and black-mailers — just like you do. That it would be better to die than to give in to them."

"In spite of the books and teachers?"

"They wrote the books and the teachers joined — they're bound to talk that way. It is propaganda — one big lie on top of the next."

"It would be easier to join. They are too big to beat!"

"Never – not even if you do."

"Good boy – man, I think." He walked over, slapped his son's back as he smiled with pride. "But do not antagonize them – it can only mean more trouble."

"They ganged up on me tonight – with knives and clubs. They said if you didn't join they'd kill me or the girls tomorrow – that they weren't going to be patient any longer. I'm not afraid, though – they've talked like that before."

Heinrich's frown was black, his face pale down to the red tinge that spread on his neck, suffused blotchily through the dark stubble. "Good God, why must you try me so!" he cried. "Is it not enough to torture me – can't you make them leave my children unharmed?"

"Now father. Please, dad – don't worry. I knew I shouldn't have told you."

"You will stay home – you will not leave this house until this is over and done."

"Never. They would brand me a coward – chicken."

"Wise men do not note this. Fools rush into traps at such bait. It is like the red cape that lures the bull to his destruction. Pay no heed. Obey my command."

"No."

"You shall. I order you not to set foot –" there was a demanding pounding at the door. "Perhaps it is over now. Perhaps they have come." He rose, walked, white-faced and tense, towards the door. He checked the chain within, twisted the latch, swung the door against the protecting links of bronze. His straight shoulders slumped, his tense face broke into a grin as he recognized the face that peered into the narrow slot. Pushing the door shut, he slipped the chain from its retainer, swung the door wide.

"Gelda," he greeted. "Gelda, how is you, man? Annie —" he yelled, "Gelda is here." His tone softened. "Sit, we will make coffee." He turned to the door, dropped the chain back into place, shot the bolt, tried it for security. "Now," he said, "how is Tar?"

"Bad. I come from the hospital. He is bad. They take skin off legs and back to put on the face and hands. They say he maybe lives, but looks different. And Paul, my little Paul—" her eyes were brimming. "Paul is low. The police do nothing — they say they have no evi — proof — who it was, that we cannot even say who we know it was because we are against the law if we accuse them. So they go on and kill more!" The last few words were hysterically sobbed as she collapsed on the couch, her body racked as Annie sat beside her, trying to offer comfort and sympathy.

"I told him to join them," she wailed. "I begged him. Told him to fight was stupid, that he could live happy if he gave in, that he would die if he did not."

"It is better to die than to become a murderer."

"That is what he said. Men are so stupid. How will I raise my children?"

"I agree with Heinrich," Annie told her. "To become a thief, a criminal, it is worse than to maybe die."

"The Kaiser killed my father in the war," Gelda moaned. "Am I now to loose my husband and son to these?"

"If it is God's will, Gelda. We do not know what He may do — we can only do what we know is right. To join them we know is wrong."

"Annie, help her to bed — she is in no condition to argue, much less to go home." He nodded his approval as his wife guided the hysterical woman to the stairs, soon he heard the creaking of the old springs intermingled with the moans and sobs.

He heard something else — furtive steps on the porch.

He picked up the phone – this was a matter for the police. He put it to his ear to see that the party line was clear; there was no sound – no conversation, no electrical buzz; the phone had been cut outside. He hurled the useless instrument from him, strode to the door, his shoulders rigid, his head erect. It was time for a showdown, at that. These men were worse than killers of children, worse than thieves – they were cowards! And cowards that they were, even in mobs they would flinch from courage.

He silently, stealthily slid the chain and bolt free, twisted the knob slowly, swung the door open with a violence that slammed it resoundingly into the wall, that propelled one of the five men huddling on the porch completely into the room.

"Ha, Ciracchi," he shouted. "Come in! Come in Ciracchi, sample my German hospitality. You, all of you, come in from the night air."

"Ha," Ciracchi snarled, as the others entered, almost sheepishly.

"Friends. All my friends. All my fellow workers and neighbors! Join me in coffee, perhaps. You, Lutz. You look shivering. Annie, Annie, the coffee for my good friends. My good friends who stand bashfully on the porch, lest they disturb me by their knock. I bring them in, I give them welcome if they do not so much for me."

"You have been offered our welcome," Ciracchi hissed. "Often you have been offered, but *you* are too good for us. No, you cut our throat, you starve our children."

"Mine eat on the same, with fare that makes them healthy. My boy – he can outwork you all, and with me."

"Scum. You lie."

"And you too much take advantage of the hospitality of my house."

"A last request. You will join us."

"A request? Ha, an order, rather. Never will I kill and plunder. Never will I shame my wife, my children with innocent blood, with wanton destruction, with loafing in mobs. You, Ciracchi, your children would better fare if you left alone the lottery. You, Lutz, you would more prosper if you worked for a living, instead of stealing it from the man who pays you to receive nothing. You—you could drive an older car and paint your house that falls to toothpicks."

"Tarnowski—remember Tarnowski and join us."

"I do not dirty the friendship I respect. For Tarnowski, if not for me, no. 'No.' Again I say no! Leave me alone, tend your affairs as I do mine, and prosper as I do."

"Fool!" You and Tarnowski—both fools. You will join —why not easily for you, by asking?"

"Out. Out, all of you! I am angered; you will fear— not me—if you remain. Out!" He collapsed, face white and drawn, as the jeering, threatening mob slammed the door behind them, jarring the ancient framework, splattering the floor with aged putty from the rattling window.

"They are gone," Annie murmered consoling. "Go to bed, father. Here, let me help you." She caught his arm, led him carefully up the open stairwell.

*   *   *   *

Fearful of lights lest they give an alarm, Heinrich edged down the stairs, hugging the wall and testing each of the dry, creaky treads before he put his weight down. The old gun, a thirty-two revolver taken on a loan to a friend, had never been used; rusty and grimy, had lain in the bedroom these many years. Now he clutched at it as a companion in the danger ahead; a creaking, furtive hint on the porch had warned him of a nocturnal visitation. He jumped at a sound behind him.

"Son get back to bed," he hissed at the young apparition who stood behind him, baseball bat gripped menacingly.

"I'm with you, Dad," came a whispered refusal.

For the second time tonight, he slid the bronze chain silently back, cautiously unlatched the knob, braced to swing the door abruptly to the surprise of intruders. The door opened, he thrust the pistol forward, into the garish, enveloping, searing blast of orange flame that leapt from the paintless porch floor.

He felt the shrapnel of shredded window glass knife into his arm and abdomen as the blast shock wave hurled him backwards into the living room, heard screams from the bedrooms upstairs. Catching his balance as he bounded from the rear wall, he staggered blindly forward, his attention divided between the licking yellow flames on the front of the house, and concern for the boy who lay soundless, still, on the living room floor. Already, sirens wailed in the distance – someone had given the alarm; help, thank God, was on the way. On the way, but the flames – they raced against the fire trucks, were eating huge black patches of porch, filling the house with smoke, encroaching on the carpet.

With one hand he jabbed the protruding intestine back into the hole in his belly, with the other, he beat feebly at the lapping flames as he died.

_ _ _ _ _ _

chapter

one

The indolent Carribean swells matched my mood as the LOAFALONG glided almost due east. To the left, just beyond the horizon, lay Key West; somewhere ahead, the Windward Passage, and my destination – an islet in the Bahamas. The bow of my eighty-five footer – once an Air-Sea Rescue boat – cut a clean white-edged vee in the transparent azure water, while the wake creaming away from the stern added the only measure of motion to the scene; without it, the boat and sea could have been a canvas, with all animation suspended forever by the painter's hand.

I almost wished the moment were frozen into permanence; after the last few jobs a rest was due. Rough ones – nothing but rough ones for the last couple of years and somehow the gun-toting living kept getting in the way of my pursuit of the historic dead. The ocean floors hold but little terror for me; nothing to compare to the black muzzle of a hood's leveled automatic.

Well below, as I lounged on the flying bridge helmsman's bench, big diesels surged and roared, but here their song was a muted purr. In the wheelhouse, I knew, there was action, the wheel-watch swinging his wheel to follow the compass card, my mate checking charts and gear – there's always work on a boat, but it was going smoothly without me. Good crew. Red Price, a transplanted Ohioan who'd adopted – and been adopted by – the Bayou people when he'd been stationed in the Cajun country during World War II; the Pollack, my kid tender – I'd been pretty lucky in getting this bunch. And Cookie, who – I reminded myself hungrily – should have chow ready pretty soon.

My lazy gaze changed to an annoyed stare; the occasional glint of sun on the back face of the long swells was out of place where the sea was broken into a regular geometric pattern of sheen and matte. Could be a shallow spot – but I was too far from shoals. Or flotsam in the water. I fixed binoculars on the flash, but lengthy study revealed no more than my initial glance – simply a glint of sun on sea ... where there should be no sheen.

I pressed the buzzer button on the speaking tube. "Red," I called, "can you come up here?"

"With or without the bottle?" a happy voice queried. "Silly question, boss; we'll be right with you."

Moments later the huge Irishman clammered onto the bridge, a fifth of Old Taylor clutched under a massively muscled arm. I pointed silently to the fleck far to the right, waited while he squinted, then grabbed the glasses. He dropped them, shrugging. "What do you make of it, Skipper?" he demanded.

"Don't know, Red. Should we check it out?"

"Doubt it," he answered. "Likely an orange crate or something as useful. You're the boss, though."

"Let's find out, I'm curious, and it's close enough.

Besides — where else do we have to go?"

"According to you, to the Bahamas. An artist's colony just reeking with women and good whiskey. Remember? Or is that another of the famous Tyler myths?" My mate grinned a toothy smile. "There ain't no women riding that old orange crate, skipper."

"So we'll be an hour later..."

"You got no idea how far I can get in an hour." Price shrugged, whistled sharply into the speaking tube. "Hey, Pollack," he called. "Swing about thirty south — steer on that fruit box the sun lights off and on."

"Wheel aye," the tube replied thinly as the ship shuddered, swayed slightly, and steadied into a long turn. The Pollack overshot, possibly not seeing our objective, caught it, and corrected his course. I took the offered bottle, and let a slug gurgle down my long immunized throat, then passed it back to my mate as I watched the spot of light grow ahead of the LOAFALONG'S bow. Finally I raised the binoculars again, studied the growing speck at length and handed them to Price. He eyed the scene briefly, then dropped the glasses with a snarl.

"Damn you, Skipper — you attract women like a Road picture does Lamour. But that one won't be worth much from the looks of things." He handed me the glasses, shourted into the tube again. "Steady on it, Pollack. Call the kid — it's a life raft and we'll go alongside."

The raft grew rapidly, in minutes the details stood out starkly; the white balsa and canvas contraption bobbing on the crests of the gentle swells, the two limp forms huddled in it, the sharp black triangles circling endlessly around it, leaving tiny wakes — the ugly dorsal fins of hopeful sharks.

"Tell Pollack not to pull alongside, Red," I said quickly. "Might upset it and give the brutes a feed.

Stand off—and bring up a couple of rifles."

"Right, Skipper." Red swung his huge bulk down the ladder with the facility of an athlete while I watched the raft's details loom bigger. There was a name on the side, but sloshing waves obscured it. The bodies—I assumed—were nearly naked and burned scarlet from the tropical sun that had blazed contunuously for weeks of a summer unbroken by cloud or rain.

One was a male, a boy in his teens I guessed; the other a girl perhaps a few years older, though the condition of both left little basis for estimate. The girl's hair, long and blonde—or brine-bleached—lay askew on the gunwale of the raft, with her neck bent sharply against it. She wore only panties or a bikini segment, and the boy was clothed in a tee shirt and swim trunks.

Neither showed sign of life as our vessel raced towards them. Below, the Pollack clutched out the pair of diesels and throttled back. The LOAFALONG rolled a bit as she coasted through the sea, slowing gradually to stop thirty or forty yards from the raft. I swung down the ladder to deck.

"Here, Skipper," Red said grimly, handing me a thirty-thirty rifle, mate to the one he cradled. Like all my guns it was loaded—an empty gun or camera is worthless in a pinch. I sighted at a spot just below a cruising dorsal as I thumbed back the hammer, and squeezed off a shot. The shark jumped nearly clear of the surface, blood pouring from entry and exit holes in his broad back, tinging the crystalline water around him with crimson. There was a flurry of indecision in the shark pack, then they rushed their injured companion, slashing with knife-edge teeth.

The shark leapt again, his tail streaming ribbons of tissue, fell among the pack. Sight of him was obscured by the threshing bodies; more blood floes drifted as the pack ripped each other while they fought for their damaged companion only themselves to become victims.

Red's rifle cracked, adding our own damage to the cannibal's decimations. A shark took off in panic; we gunned him. He rolled a white belly upwards, doubling completely. We plunked more lead into him as he lay, then picked new targets as a part of the survivors in the shoal fell upon him. My hammer clicked on an empty chamber, I grabbed the hot barrel and fed the magazine from a cartridge box Red had dropped on deck. Snapping the lever, I threw more lead into the water now tinged a uniform red pastel.

The boat lurched, making sternway to stay near the raft as my kid tender joined the shooting party armed with an automatic twenty-two—not likely to kill one of the brutes, but capable of making the blood crazed pack attack and do the job themselves. On we went, firing at any possible target, a few bullets richcheting from the smooth planes of the sea to whine away like sound effects in a Western movie. Abrupt silence fell; the red sea was empty!

"Red. Kid," I said, "rig the cargo boom. As bad shape as they're in, we'd better try to lift the raft aboard if either are alive." I dropped my rifle, walked to the fan tail lifelines and stepped across.

"Good Gawd, Skipper," Red shouted, "you aren't going to swim to the raft with the sea full of sharks!"

"We've routed the critters, Red. You two can shoot any that come back—which you'll not likely have to do. And I don't know a case of sharks attacking a fully dressed swimmer."

"What part of your clothes will scare 'em?" the kid grinned. "The yacht cap, or the Hawaiian print whatchacallem—loincloth?"

"Sarong. A male answer to Dorothy Lamour. And I should have fired you last trip." I laughed. "Let's get with it." With more trepidation than I admitted, I tilted into a long racing dive. The brine closed tepidly about me. Straightening, I stroked a few times, breaking water halfway to the raft.

A few fast strokes brought me in and I dragged myself carefully over the end, in a low crouch to avoid undue tipping. A glance around revealed no cruising sharks; perhaps we'd be spared more of that. My stomach turned; a sweeping wave of nausea gripped me as I looked at the boy. No question there; he'd been dead in this blazing sun much too long! I braced myself, held my breathing to a minumum, turning my head windward when I had to gasp in a lungful of air.

Something had gotten to him—sharks or shrimp or small feeding fish—where he'd slept or died with an arm hanging out of the raft. I tried to reach for him, but my arms refused the task. Bracing myself hard against revulsion, nausea, and breathlessness, I caught him and began to heave, but stopped short of the gunwale. In his back, nearly centered, was the entry wound, small and round, a blue rimmed black hole with a bit of adhering congealed blood. I dropped him back into the raft—a shipwreck victim can be buried at sea, but not the victim of a murderer!

Washing my hands in the sea I turned my attention to the girl. As I'd surmised, she was older—probably in her twenties. She'd been beautiful—a blonde about five-feet six, and perfectly proportioned. Now the firm breasts were cooked to an angry red like all the rest exposed to the weather. There was no decompostion, though, and I stared hard, doubting as an illusion that her chest had fluttered.

Dropping an ear to a breast I felt the soaked up heat, felt the baked skin flake under the touch—but heard a distant heartbeat! I listened intently; the beat was faint but regular. Rising with a sense of urgency I waved the boat towards me, saw the boom swinging across the side, a steel cable harness already rigged to the weighted winch hook. I caught the hook with difficulty; the LOAFALONG rolled lazily while I bobbed on the crests of the waves. Everytime I reached, the elusive hook swung clear of my grasp.

Finally I secured the cables under the ends of the balsa boat and, standing with hand on hook, motioned the kid to lift away. The raft swung over the water, spun a few times despite my steadying grip, then smacked back momentarily as the big boat heeled in the trough. Again it rose, swinging wildly in over the lifelines, across the deck. Red caught the gunwale to steady it as the kid dropped it gently onto the planks, sliding the winch brake to spool off bare inches each time.

"Call the Coast Guard, Red," I directed, "Tell them we've victims of the..." I glanced at the neat black letters on the raft, "Motor Yacht VOLSTOK II, one of whom is alive and suffering from exposure. Get directions for feeding and handling. I'll take her down below. Get a bottle of Vasolene out of the chest, I know we'll need that." I heard air hiss, the clutches on the engines slam home. The Pollack was putting way on the boat to check the roll. "Kid..." I stopped, he was already unrolling a stretcher.

We had to take the stretcher through the cockpit, engine room, and galley; it wouldn't make the corners from the wheelhouse down. Gently I laid the girl on a clean sheet, took the bottle of petrolatum that the kid offered, and began rubbing it into her cooked skin, flicking my hands to throw off hard parchment patches that slithered off as I worked with the grease. I hardly regarded her as a girl as my hands touched her body — she was that bad!

"They say nothing but orange juice," Red said, extending a cup half full. "And only a little of that. The vasolene's okay and let her lie and rest — they're trying to arrange to send a doctor out by chopper and asked if we could get into Sarasota or Tampa with her if they decided not to take her off immediately."

"Tell them yes — wherever they say. Give Pollack the course." I cradled the blonde head in one arm, set the glass gently against her lips, and coaxed some of the juice down her throat. She seemed to swallow slightly; little by little the level dropped until I set aside the empty glass.

"Skipper," Red bellowed from the wheelhouse, "they want you on the horn." I pulled a sheet over the girl, clambered up the ladder, and took the phone he extended. "Gaylord," he explained. Gaylord — manager of the New Orlean's regional office of Laird's; one of the biggest casualty insurers in the world. I'd worked for him on salvage jobs, and had indirectly gotten him his job — but was puzzled by his calling now.

"Tyler," I said into the microphone.

"Tyler, this is Lloyd Gaylor. I understand you've picked up survivors from the VOLSTOK."

"One survivor. Other dead."

"Have you heard about the sinking?"

"Negative."

"Fill you in. VOLSTOK II is owned by the Harrison family here — that's *THE* Harrison's — Rick and Emily, who give the city a new park and swimming pool every year to cut their income tax bill. They were cruising the Carribean — island hopping — for a couple of months, and were on their way back when the sinking occurred. Skipper was found in a lifeboat, chugging along with an outboard motor, and was brought in by a Jap freighter — the IPPUCU MARU — and dropped by lighter at Satasota, Florida. He's under sedation and observation at the hospital there — needlessly, I think: he's as well off as if he'd been on a day-rental-fishing bit. Tells quite a story. Cruising along when he hit a squall. Everything open, people lounging on deck, all the hatches gaping. Caught one over the shoulder, floundered and sank almost instantly. Found himself swimming, latched onto the drifting boat, and headed for home after an unsuccessful search for survivors. Rescued after three days — had been sailing with a shirt on a paddle until it ripped out, then he started the kicker hoping it'd take him into shipping lanes where he'd be sighted. As happened, of course."

"One victim is shot — not exposed," I interjected.

"God, no!" Gaylord exclaimed. "Try to keep that from the papers. Take over that end for us, will you — try to get a statement from the survivor if she — it was the girl, wasn't it? — regains consciousness. Have a police guard posted wherever they take her — hospital, I suppose. We'll guarantee all costs. Can you handle it?"

"I've a hot date in the Bahamas, fella — gal I haven't seen for a couple of years and keep trying to drop in on. And been promising myself a vacation all that time. Rather leave it to you and the Coast Guard; it's not my baby."

"You get a pile of work from us, Tyler. And owe us a favor to two as well as the converse. We can't manage to get anyone else on the scene quickly; you're already there."

"You win. But I'll double my usual rates right down the line, Gaylord — though it still won't be enough compensation for missing the Bahamas. You'd agree if you saw her."

"Fine." He laughed. "But we may argue your statement down to half the usual — the ship, passengers — we carry insurance on everything connected with them so it'll cost enough without you salting the mine."

"Want to keep the phone open for the Coast Guard, Gaylord. I'll call later, soon as there's something new.

Tyler and LOAFALONG, over and out." I dropped the handset, glanced at the compass with a nod. We were headed for Tampa.

_ _ _ _

chapter
two

The small wake was of turgid mud as I tooled the LOAFALONG up a canal meant for outboard-fishing boats. It was grueling work, inching ahead, eyes fixed on banks a dozen feet on each side of my boat's broad beam, juggling throttles and wheels to fend against a light crosswind. With too little power, the ship swung towards the port bank, with too much the froth behind was beat into a chocolaty-batter by the big props that swung bare inches above the bottom of the drainage slash that connected a Sarasota Marina with a now distant Gulf of Mexico.

Janice Harrison still lay on the bunk below, tended by a doctor dropped from a clamorous Marine helicopter some hours before. She was still in coma, but after adrenalin and a dozen other shots, along with intravenous feeding, her heartbeat was stronger, and breath obvious, if shallow. The putrescent corpse had — thank God — been canvas wrapped and taken off by the rescue crew on the 'copter; I'd only with difficulty managed to toss a blanket over it where it lay in the salvaged raft. Another call to Laird's had laid a groundwork for me — gotten the canal cleared of traffic, an ambulance standing by at the Marina, a rental car delivered, and accomodations reserved at the Mecca — (this in Florida?) Motel. The Miami office, in charge in this district, was also sending a rep over to help me, as required. A gust swung the bow — I jammed on throttle and rudder, veered towards, then away from the bank, spun the wheel and throttles to break an overcompensation, and finally steadied in the canal again, feeling a bit shaky; this trip was torture.

"Starboard, quick," Red snapped from my shoulder; unquestioning I put the wheel over, throttled hard and sent the big boat careening to within inches of the bank as a speedhull running flat out on its sixty-horsepower engine whined past to port. He was making an easy thirty-five miles an hour, spray obscuring his forward vision, his bow wave curling a yard above the gunwales of the low, squat hull. He smacked into the turbulence of my bow, wavered, slewed wildly as he overcontrolled, fighting to steady on his course.

A hundred yards ahead he hit the bank obliquely, knifed up the palmetto and grass covered bank, jumped the top of the ridge and tore on across the flats towards highway 41 and a roadside grocery. He'd released the wheel, and was gesticulating wildly, the engine snapped up to tote position, continued to scream at an unloaded top speed far beyond its design.

The boat crashed into a palmetto clump, hurling him out and over into the sharp, hard frounds, and the engine — probably breaking a piston or two — stopped with a crash of backfiring. Concerned, I watched, but the kid — somewhere in his early twenties at the top, picked himself, clothes streaming, from the thicket to stand waving his fist at me beside the wreckage of his boat.

Price bellowed, "That crazy bastard — mad at us when he should have been taking the channel at ten miles top. And what about the Coast Guard — they were supposed to have had it cleared!"

"Likely he lived along it somewhere, and dropped his boat between blocks. I suppose he'll try to collect damages from me yet, after endangering my boat with his screwball performance. Sort of hope so; I'd like to tell him what I think of his kind."

"Yeah," the kid interjected. "Private pleasure boating is getting a black eye and getting loaded down with restrictions too because of his breed. Damned people ought to be hung at the yardarm. Rep's even carrying over to the professional boatmen; we'll all suffer in the long run for it. If he comes over to cry on our shoulders I'd like an invite to the party too."

"Welcome to the party. Come as you are." I broke off conversation as the bridge carrying the Tamiami Trail loomed ahead, the boatyard – Marina to the right below it. Red and the kid joined the Pollack on the deck to handle lines; I swung the LOAFALONG up to the rough timber pier, backing down so close that they stepped across with their lines.

In the boatyard, pandemonium raged. Men in white coats, in blue and grey police uniforms, in Coast Guard uniforms, and in business suits, men with cameras and men with briefcases, tall and short and handsome and homely men, pushed, jostled, and gave conflicting orders as Cookie reduced the din only modestly by shutting down the throbbing diesels below. There were ambulances and cars with doctor's emblems, cars with press stickers, and cars with manned TV cameras on their roofs.

Someone should have been selling hot dogs and balloons.

The ambulance, siren making little moaning sounds, inched its way through the pack while what I'd identified as Sarasota cops tried to tie a guard line twenty feet up the bank to restrain the mob. Despite the police and the ambulance, the first man to hit my deck carried a Graphic.

I promptly forgot the name he announced proudly, and even the paper's identity, told him to get ashore, that any statement would be delayed, and would come from authoritative sources. He crowded me momentarily, then backed off as Red's massive bulk interposed and pressed him inexorably back to shore.

The ambulance attendants boarded, hauled their patient and her attendant doctor off in the ambulance, and the law, finally controlling the mob, waved a trio of men, two uniformed, past the cordon. The civilian led the procession to the fantail, stepped aboard, and offered hand and business card simultaneously.

"Jay Redmond, Laird's Miami," he snapped off. "Glad to meet you, Tyler. You're a bit of a legend around our office — in fact — through the company after the Goldbaum affair." His grin twisted downward. "Not a legend with a happy ending, you understand."

"Welcome aboard, Mr. Redmond," I acknowledged.

"And meet Coast Guard Ensign, Garrity, and Sergeant Mulforn of the Sarasota PD, Identification Section."

"Pleasure, Ensign, Sergeant. Come down to the lounge where we can escape —" I waved shoreward — "the TV and newshawks. I'll introduce you to the crew too, when they're through battling would-be boarders."

Mulforn grinned. "More excitement than when the circus comes to town," he said, "especially since the biggest of them winters here. You're in the big middle of making news on a world-wide basis; you'll understand better when we've filled you in."

I gestured. They followed me through the wheelhouse, down the steep ladder, and into the lounge.

Redmond surveyed the compartment and whistled at the long bar, vinyl tile deck, comfortable couches and indirect lights. "Hi-fi, yet," he muttered, "didn't expect to find a ballroom on a salvage boat."

"The boat – an*d* salvage for that matter – is more hobby than business," I explained. "And sometimes I have to entertain aboard. Business contacts, you understand."

"Yeah – I understand," he laughed. "And I assume *you* give *them* the business. A T-Bird is the best cat wagon I've been able to manage on my salary."

"So why work for a living," I said. "I gave it up long ago. Oh, meet my crew – " I added as Red, the kid, and Cookie entered. I made the introduction, Red reported that the crowd was dissipating, but he'd have to help the Pollack with reporters, and motioned the group back to deck.

"Small crew for so big a vessel," Garrity remarked. you came under regulations as a carrier, you'd have to triple the number."

"On rough jobs I pick up one or two more," I explained. "And most of the maintenance is done in shipyards, so we get along well enough. No one's worked too hard, and it's cheaper to contract a load than to keep hands aboard. Besides, I'm touchy about reliability – getting a big crew with the versatility, loyalty and discretion of this bunch is out of the question."

"I understand that discretion part," Garrity responded. "Trying to pry anything out of your crew is hopeless – it's been tried a time or two when we got to wondering about you. And the record pages are still a blank. There was something about an airplane we thought carried a bunch of revolutionaries once. We nailed the plane after weeks of stake-outs, and seized a load of stale mullet . . . "

"And shook my crew down because I'd been cruising in the neighborhood the day before." I shrugged. "The ocean's still free—I don't have to account for my whims."

"You will someday!" Garrity's eyes snapped, his voice was razoredged. "We know they got in and back out with a load of American munitions; guns, cartridges, uniforms—a whole damned shipload of contraband."

"Really," Redmond interjected. "No recriminations, please, gentlemen. We've important—and current affairs to deal with."

"And we'll deal with them without the Coast Guard's aid if this joker makes me throw him overboard," I snapped.

"You'll have to call your crew!" My hand snapped forward, seized his tie and uniform shirt front. I jerked him towards me; he lost balance as I shoved backwards and released my grip. Staggering a few steps, he crashed onto a couch. As he struggled to get to his feet, I rushed, only to be caught short in a vise grip of the policeman.

"Easy, Tyler," he admonished.

"It's my ship—I'll throw this wisecracking bastard overboard whenever I want," I snapped. "I can deal with Coast Guard officers, but a damned ninety-day ensign coming aboard and wising off is too much..."

The ensign lunged. Redmond, smallest in the group, blocked him easily. "Cool off," Redmond admonished. "Tyler's right; you've little basis for coming aboard his vessel and starting a row. Also, he's here on behalf of Laird's, acting as agent for us in this matter. I've instructions to supply any and all assistance —but to act under his orders."

"You mean he can boss an assistant regional manager?" Garrity asked with obvious surprise.

"Yes."

"I was out of line, Tyler. I'm sorry. Actually, I started out kidding without knowing I was rubbing the wrong way. Mostly kidding, anyhow. There *are* things we'd like to know about your operations." He extended a hand, I took it.

"Allright," Redmond sighed, "let's get down to business, Tyler. I understand you have none of the story except your end?"

"About it," I agreed. "Except what Gaylord sketched on the radiophone."

"I'll give you a complete dossier on the Harrison's, on the skipper — a Grissolm — and the boat survey records. Roughly, here it is; We carried all the family policies and insurance on the VOLSTOK — documented as a yacht, incidentally — life, jewelry, the works, so we'd be into it for a pile however you figure it. But worse, Emily Harrison had wanted her Nassau jeweler to appraise some stones she'd taken on approval from a New York house."

"Necklace and pendant with a pear cut seven-carat stone and about forty little ones, a couple of bracelets — altogether we carried a valuation of one hundred eighty thousand on the package. Guess she and we had rocks in our heads; they should have been courier-carried for appraisal, but the VOLSTOK was a sound ship and the family completely responsible, so we let her take them along. They had hired the skipper — and we missed the boat there, too — we assumed they had checked him out. On the face of it, he's a competent seaman, but on investigation, he's either accident-prone or pretty rugged. He hasn't a thing against him — no convictions, no fines, no warnings, but listen:" He pulled a sheet from his sheaf, began reading:

"1947 — Lost charter boat he owned. Boat was swept into an offshore oil rig — abandoned and unlighted despite the regulations—in heavy weather. Insured, but lightly. Lost his wife in that sinking. She was insured too. Heavily.

"1948—Crashed and wiped out a DC3 airliner owned by Foothills, and bought war surplus to refit for scheduled airline service. Ran out of fuel in fog and sleet, after radioing that his receiver had failed, and he presumed he was off course. Yeah—he has a pilot's license and ATR as well as his maritime ticket—real smart boy, I'd say. The airplane was heavily insured—carried the figure normal for airline equipment though it had been bought surplus for a song. He was cleared—mostly on the basis of known bad weather, and his radioed claim that his beam receiver was out.

"1952. Lost fifty-four foot charter boat. Engine room explosion and flash fire. There were two deaths in that one. He was salaried—no apparent gain.

"1958. Piled an inter-island freighter onto a reef off Andros Island in the Bahamas group. The inquiry really ripped him over that—four days of interrogation. But he was cleared. Seems like a drunk seaman had wheel watch and ran off course so far during the night that they hadn't had any warning. The skipper was off watch when the freighter piled in and tore her bottom out.

"That was his last responsible job until he hired out to skipper the VOLSTOK—he doesn't have any discernable employment history in the interim, but probably was living on the investment proceeds of his insurance checks."

"Looks as though his record's no longer conviction free," I said. "He's sure to be tagged for murder this time, judging from his story and from the murdered kid I hauled in. By the way," I glanced at the policeman, "does he know about the raft yet?"

"No. We put a police guard on him at once. No visitors are permitted, and he'll have no papers or news reports. We have the girl under guard too — obviously for different reasons."

"I'd like to quiz the skipper about his position and the sinking generally before anyone can get the news to him," I suggested.

"We could arrange it; I could go along with you. Not that we normally invite outsiders into things of this sort, but the chief passed the word to extend every courtesy."

"Thanks. I'll take you up on it."

"I understand," Redmond interrupted, "that you'll be primarily interested in locating the vessel, if possible, in salvaging the gems if they are still aboard and in checking any evidence that might indicate barratry — or otherwise affect our settlement."

"Thanks for the reminder."

Redmond looked disconcerted. I laughed at his discomfort. "But I'm fairly familiar with my functions. And frequently I've found more profitable information sources ashore than undersea. Also, the oceans are pretty big places; it's easier to start hunting for a wreck in a bar or a hospital room than in a million square mile blank of salt water. I'll study your reports and dossiers, talk to the skipper, the girl when and if she comes around, and maybe some family and friends in the next few days. Wrecks don't go anywhere; people do — especially if they feel guilty. Then we'll decide on trying to locate the vessel — there's no point in billing your company for going off on a tangent and searching two oceans for nothing."

"I see. Gaylord told me you didn't work according to books or job descriptions. Guess I'll have to simply stand by with an offer of any aid possible, including, of course, our investigative and adjustment section."

"Good. Can't think of anything at the moment — I

may after I digest your data. Meanwhile," I glanced at the sergeant, "could we talk to Grissolm?"

"Yes," Mulforn replied. "I'll clear it with the office by phone. We can take my car down to the hospital — you probably aren't familiar with the city?"

"Only on US 41, I'm afraid. Appreciate it." We said our goodbyes, I accompanied the officer to his radio car. He drove expertly in the going-home traffic, occasionally making a hole in an incipient traffic tangle with an impatient growl of his siren. In minutes he swung into an 'official car' parking slot; we made our way to an accident ward. The patrolman at the second floor door saluted, a few words were exchnaged, his face brightening with the thought of relief from duty for a few minutes, then we entered the private room.

Chester M. Grissolm was young for his experiences- perhaps under forty. He was a couple of inches under the six-foot mark, and retained a good build, though thickening around the middle a bit. Uniformly tanned, his blue eyes crinkled in the corners, symptomatic of an outdoor life, and the constant squint against flaring ocean suns.

"Grissolm," Mulforn nodded, keeping his voice carefully neutral, "This is Jeff Tyler, a salvage diver who's going to hunt for the VOLSTOK. I brought him up to discuss your — mishap — you might be able to help him spot the wreckage."

"Pleasure," Grissolm muttered, his voice firm but disinterested. "But it's hopeless. We went down in the slot — deeps off New Providence. No chance of locating the boat, less of getting down to it."

I shrugged. "Rough all over these days. What really happened?"

"What little there is to tell, the papers got long ago," he said. "Squall hit us off the islands. We were in the slot, heading for Miami to fuel and supply for the run around the Keys to New Orleans. Had been island hopping all over the Carribean for a couple of months. Sea came over the starboard quarter and swamped us instantly. Washed most of the family off the deck, trapped the rest below decks I suppose. I was on the flying bridge. Dumped me into the drink. Swam until I ran across the dingy and rigged a sail on it. Cruised around the area but didn't find any survivors — wasn't surprised at that. Wind carried me a couple of days, finally my jury-rigged sail and shirt gave out so I drifted until I figured the outboard might take me into the shipping lanes. Just lucky guesswork there; I had nothing to navigate with. It did — a Jap freighter brought me on in."

He paused. I glanced at Mulforn, got a barely perceptible nod. "Could you give me the position at the time of sinking?"

"Within maybe ten miles. I'd set course for Miami, had a long trip ahead, and didn't bother — who does? — with running chart positions. Hell, I was enjoying the cruise too."

"Jan and Dick Harrison's evidence doesn't agree with yours, Skipper," I said casually, my voice carefully flat. The man's transition was abrupt, his face turned white, then greenish, his jaw and cheeks distorted, he half-started from the bed. "I brought them in, you see." I explained as flatly.

For a long moment he stared at my face, either trying to decide that I was lying, or too incredulous to think at all. His stare changed to one of partial comprehension, then his eyes widened again, mad with realization and terror as a vast blow on the head hurled me forward towards his inane features. I saw Mulforn, also hurled forward, a stare of torture on his face. The pain of the massive attack caught me in a flash of blinding crimson that wavered, interspersed with flaming yellows and deathly blacks. The blacks blotted the pyrotechnics; I felt myself falling. Then nothing.

------

chapter
three

Consciousness returned gradually like a trickle of water dripping into a dry lake bed that fills almost imperceptibly. There was no 'on or off' function; just a gradual awareness that I *was*. Pain began later, with its surging crimson and yellow flames that ate into my awareness, but sharpened one little corner. I could see nothing, but distant voices made a cacophony that distracted my efforts at reason. Pain flared and the blackness again tried to engulf me, but didn't quite. I tried to move an arm, found it restrained. Sensations were returning; I felt a sharp jab, and shortly a warmness throughout. Voices were clearer, I distinguished both male and female. Again I tried to see — this time realizing that I had first to open my eyes.

"He's conscious!" a voice exclaimed nearby.

"Don't disturb him!" another admonished.

"When will he talk," demanded a third. This one was tense.

"Aukawageekee," I muttered. It wasn't what I'd planned on saying. In fact, it sounded silly. I tried harder. To ask where I was would seem melodramatic. Pulling myself together I made another effort. It came out as badly.

"Concussion possibly. We'll have to watch—may re-
quire trephine..." I heard a competent voice reflect.
Damned if I'd have them putting a silver plate in my
hard skull!

"What time is it?" I finally managed.

"Seven twenty-three," a nurse replied. I focused my
eyes on her, wished I hadn't. Maybe I was dead and in
hell, with one of Lucifer's consorts holding my wrist.
Seven-thirty. I'd been out quite a while. Turning my
head I saw a veritable army of nurses, doctors, and
cops. I tossed my head angrily against a nurse's re-
straints, and looked further. Two more beds—besides
the one I occupied, had been crammed into the small
room. Human forms showed under them; with a shock
I saw that the sheets covered even their heads!

"For Gawd's sake, what happened?" I demanded.

"Hoped you might shed some light on that," a man
in a police lieutneant's uniform said grimly. "You're
the only one left to tell us."

I put a hand to my head; the itch persisted, unreach-
able through the swath of bandages! "Grissolm..."
I began.

"Is dead," the lieutenant informed me. "And my
man, Mulforn, is dead. So—unfortunately ,is the guy
that shot them, and you. My patrolman gunned him as
he started out of the room with a doctor's jacket on.
Somehow got by the whole damned hospital staff."
The lieutenant snatched a sheet away from the adjoining bed. "Anyone you've seen before?"

"No," I mused, studying the features. He was a smal-
lish man with a waspish expression, even in death.
His eyebrows were black and thick, chin covered with
a coarse black stubble. His hair, through years of careful marcelling, had assumed a permanent wave. I
guessed him at forty-five to fifty. "Any identification?"

"Yeah. Union card calls him Lorenzo Ippaccio, Longshoreman. Also old card in the building trades. Labor. One of your towns-people, Tyler — New Orleans."

"They aren't all knights in — turbans — " I grimaced, stroking my head again, "Sour one here or there. Transplant or visitor?"

"Visitor. Return ticket on Delta."

"Fast work, wasn't it? With the news just out this morning. Or maybe it was scheduled — could be he tried to cut the stones one way less."

"Doesn't seem likely — too pat. Must have been news of the pickup you made."

"How's Janice?"

"Coming along nicely, they think. Doctors say she'll probably regain consciousness soon, and we'll want to interview her as soon as possible."

"Hope she's well enough guarded."

"You can bet on that." An expression of pain crossed the cop's sharp face. "We've got half the force on that one."

"I'll want to represent Laird's at the interview, Lieutneant."

"If you don't let a gunny follow you in, I suppose. Hell — I can't hold it against you. It was my sergeant who relieved the hall watch — wouldn't have happened if he hadn't given the man a coffee break."

I struggled to a sitting position, threw my legs from the bed as the hospital staff rushed me. I waved them off, stood. All the strength drained from me; I collapsed on the floor, making excuses as clucking nurses dragged me back onto the bed.

"Don't try that again," the doctor admonished. "If you want to live. The bullet cut a furrow across the top of your head — a thirty-eight slug from a silenced automatic. There may be concussion — you'll have to stay here a day or two at least." He turned to a nurse, whispered instructions. The nurse scampered away. "You can't take injuries like this lightly, Tyler."

"I've a job to do, Doctor."

"You won't do it dead, Tyler — nor till you can stand up — why delay it with foolishness?" He took a syringe the nurse offered, plunged it into my arm. "Count backwards from ten," he suggested. I got only to seven.

The pain was still there in the morning, but I'd learned to live with it. Or closer than I could live with the sterile hospital breakfast of scrupulously dried toast, half-cooked egg in a shell, and anemic coffee. Idly I speculated on whether they'd fine Red for bringing in a flask of Old Taylor while a pair of efficient, eagle-eyed, hawk-faced nurses changed the bloody mass of dressings on my head, checked my pulse and respiration, and entered data on the chart at the foot of the bed.

"Good morning," called a voice with a bedside smile. I turned to face the doctor with a baleful glare.

"Ugh," I replied. "Five cups of coffee and a shot of good whiskey from now, I wouldn't want to smack that grin off your face."

"Maybe I *can* make you feel better, Tyler." His face sobered. "I've just come from another patient — a little blonde gal who has all kinds of bounce. Yesterday I wouldn't have bet a nickel on her, but she's awake and chipper and wants to say thanks whenever you can get free. Wait!" he ejaculted, rushing me as I swung my legs out of bed. He caught them and threw them back. "You're determined to kill yourself — let me look at your chart." He surveyed it, lips pursed. "I think you're coming along. I'll have a nurse wheel you up in a chair."

"You'll....!" I snapped. A nurse jumped, wheeled

with a look of sheer hatred, and bolted through the
door. "I'm sorry, Doc. But you won't wheel me anywhere, and especially to meet a blonde." I swung from
the bed and stood beside it, holding the cold steel rail
for balance. The room tilted sickeningly, straightened.
Releasing my hold, I took a faltering step and felt
better. "Now have them dig my clothes," I told the harried medic. "I'm going out on a hot date."

    *   *   *   *   *   *   *

I'd have liked to have shaved and changed clothes;
my jacket was a bloody mess from a bit of gunshot
hemmorhage, but there was no choice. Just getting
through the cordon of cops took most of what energy I
had; this one they weren't muffing.

Janice Harrison bore little resemblance to the girl
I'd so recently dragged from the sea. Her hair was
combed, shoulder-length, it was strewn over the pillow in a tawny spider web that caught the sunlight
from the window and refracted it prismatically. She
wore a negligee of blue silk; only her burned face and
neck reflected her ordeal visibly now. Her blistered
lips cracked into a smile as I approached.

"Miss Harrison," I said.

"Jan. And I can't give you my hand – it's wrapped
like a Cheops dynasty mummy. You're Jeff Tyler,
aren't you?" She added, as an afterthought, "the man
who dragged me out of the raft?"

"Yes. You sure look better than you did day before
yesterday, Jan. How do you feel?"

"Numb. I guess I should be shocked by – by what
happened, and sore all over too, but I'm not. Partly
sedation. Partly all the nerve ends are burned off
everywhere – they tell me I won't feel pain from the
burns for a week or two. They wanted to do some

grafting but couldn't find any skin left to work with. God, I'm a mess." She stared at me at length. "With a shave you'd look allright," she decided. "Unless—you aren't bald, are you?"

"Wasn't the last I looked. No idea what's under the turban now, myself."

"I knew you weren't—" she smiled, "or I wouldn't have been rude enough to ask. Married?"

"No."

"Odd."

"If that's a question, hell *no!*"

She laughed, a flash of pain showing in her eyes as the skin around her mouth tightened. "Okay, I asked for it. And I guess I'm stalling. I—I don't want to talk about what I know I have to talk about."

"You do, though, Jan. And you should really want to —there are the people responsible—you have to want to see them caught. We already know from where I picked you up that the skipper's story was phony—and what happened yesterday clinched that. Can you talk about the sinking—or should we give you another day or two to rest up?"

"Might as well get on with it, Jeff. Do you want it my way or would rather ask questions?"

"You tell it, Jan. I'll butt in as you go."

"What was it—six nights ago—on the seventeenth, I think. Six or seven or eight—I'm a little confused. We were headed for New Orleans after a dreamy trip all over the islands. Hardly a day of bad weather all the way, and I think—well, it was perfect. We had wondered about the captain when we'd hired him, but Chet turned out real well—though he was a bit of a wolf every time his wife's back was turned—"

"Can't blame him for that. Even in the shape you're in, you're beautiful."

She stuck her tongue out, "Or maybe he was just

male. Anyhow, we spent the evening on deck; weather was clear, with that luminosity in the sky that makes it seem — sort of sticky or thick. Tropical skies made me think of taffy for some reason. I was among the last to turn in. Eileen — that was Chet's wife — and I sat on the foredock looking at stars and talking small talk. She told me how she'd met Chet, what a bunch of raw deals he'd had, and the like. Finally we turned in too. Sometime later — I suppose it must have been one-thirty or two AM — there was all kinds of commotion on deck. I heard mother screaming, gunshots, swearing. Eileen was there too, calling Chet crazy and sounding hysterical. I had been sunning in a Bikini all afternoon, and hadn't changed, just laid down — so I pulled on a robe and rushed up on deck. I heard Dick call from behind me, and told him to come along. When I came through the wheelhouse to deck I must have fainted. God, there was blood everywhere. Chet had a rifle and a fire axe, mother and dad were sprawled on deck, Eileen...was strewn around....," Janice had paled, looking ghostly despite the angry burns; I reached for the nurse call button, but she shook her head. Closing her eyes, she shuddered, while the sheet heaved sharply over her bosom. Finally she opened her eyes. "I'm sorry. For a minute I was back...there... on deck..."

"You shouldn't even think of it, much less talk about it, right now, Jan. Wish I could spare you this." She smiled weakly, another shudder racked her, then she began more resolutely.

"Sometime — just before or after I passed out there was a break in the yacht's pace — like it had stubbed its toe. An awful grinding and grating, and the boat listed hard to port. I think I called and asked Chet if we were sinking and he'd yelled back 'Hell, Yes.'

And he was launching our dingy—the one with the outboard that we used for a shore boat. I think I saw him put spare cans of gasoline in it—or maybe I dreamt this part; I'm not sure. When we listed I rolled against Dick—he was hurt; he said he'd been shot in the back. There was blood all around and under him. I unhooked the liferaft—it had parrot clips and wasn't hard, and helped him onto it. I couldn't either launch it or get Dick into it if I had—so I sat down in it on the fantail and as the VOLSTOK got lower and lower in the water —she was settling by the bow and I was afraid suction might pull us under, but couldn't do anything about it—the raft finally floated clear. Chet had been gone a long time by then, and I hadn't found . . . ," she choked on it, "the bodies anyplace. We just drifted. A couple of times I saw boats and waved, but they didn't see me. Dick died not long after I got him into the raft, and he . . . got stiff. I couldn't push him out. By then I was hoping I'd die—it was—seemed so easy. But I was afraid to drink salt water so I just lay there waiting." Her eyes closed again; I noted with alarm her shallow breathing. Finally she recovered. "Jeff," she demanded suddenly, "what did I have on when you picked me up?"

"A Bikini bottom."

She flushed. "I'm sorry."

"I'm not. But it's a heck of a thing to worry about now. Do you have any idea of your position when you went down?"

"No."

"But you were headed for New Orleans? Grissolm said you'd been going to fuel in Miami."

"No. That's ridiculous. The VOLSTOK carried enough fuel for fifteen days continuous cruising with reserves. And we'd fueled and supplied in Nassau."

A nurse flounced in, checked Jan's pulse and temperature, told me she shouldn't be tired further, and left. I rose. "I'll have to get along before the warden cuts me down, Jan," I said. "Are you going back to New Orleans soon?"

"That's home. I'll go as soon as I'm released. They say three or four days—whenever I've put on a few pounds and gotten an appetite back. And am off this gunk they're shooting me full of."

"Well, I'll see you there if not before. Probably have to ask you to fill in some details soon."

"Damned romantic of you, Skipper," she quipped.

"Thought I might need an excuse. I'll hold it open just in case—but we may as well both concede it's an excuse."

"That's a little better, but I wouldn't have thought you'd need a crutch. Anyhow, Jeff, thanks so much for everything and I do hope I see you soon. I will recover, you know—that's more than you can say for a lobster of the same shade."

"Goodbye, Jan. I'll try to see you before you leave, but if not, I'll look you up as soon as you get back." She smiled as I turned away and headed for the Admittance Desk to sign a check for a one-night stay in a hard-mattressed bed that should have bought me a motel Beauty-Rest for a week with hot and cold running maids.

*   *   *   *

The rest of the day was spent in a round of conferences that made me realize how weak the hole in the head had left me. And all unproductive; I wound up as did the police, the Coast Guard, and the Miami branch of Laird's, as much in the dark as I'd began. The consensus was that the skipper, Chet Grissolm, had either gone berserk and turned killer, or had decided the gems were bait enough to justify mass murder and barratry. Laird's was tempted to pay off claims without contest, the police hoped to close their case by laying the whole blame on the skipper, since his killer, too, had been executed, and the Coast Guard was willing to write off the sinking as barratry by a probably insane master. To me it stank—and I practically shouted my opinion. Why would an insane man be killed the instant witnesses to his crime were located? Why would a lone wolf gem thief be? The longer we talked, the more impatient I became; there were answers. They couldn't be found here in a round of conferences. Finally—if my guesses were right, Janice Harrison would have to die. She must, to protect whatever forces closed Grissolm's mouth so permanently.

The police weren't too sure of themselves, though. They charged me as a material witness, forbade my leaving the area, or moving the LOAFALONG. There was a last conference—with my crew, which I turned loose on the town for an indeterminate leave—while I caught a charter plane to New Orleans.

– – – – –

chapter

four

Don Miller grinned from across the green felt covered table, illumined by a single hanging lamp depending from the ceiling above its shadowless center. The grin made his hook-nosed face a bit sinister; he was at his best in repose. Nearly my height, he looked smaller, his light build and long fingered, artist-like hands lent a speed in pinches that was inevitably deceptive. And damned convenient.

The hands *were* artistic; they could triple-stack a deck, snap out the second, third, or bottom card, cock and trigger a gun with deadly accuracy, or make a twenty-dollar bill or questioned document vanish without evident motion or effort. The grin was staging; his face never reflected a genuine emotion.

"Hi, Jeff, 'ole poison," he intoned. "What kind of trouble are we in this time?"

"Hell, Don. Can't I just drop in to say hello?"

"That'll be a great day. Don't mind my boys – they're familiars – go ahead and spill it."

I shrugged. "Okay. Rick and Emily Harrison, the

VOLSTOK II, and Chester Grissolm."

Don moaned. "Your cut, skipper, and include me out. I don't even want to put my change in the pot this deal."

"Old Taylor highball—double it up," I told the barmaid. "And whatever the boss is drinking."

"Same," Don told her, "since I've got a live one to pay for it. First live one this week, I think. Look, Jeff. Let me buy the drink, wish you a happy new year and send you on your way before you get me tangled up with that Harrison mess. I heard that you'd pulled the doll out of the drink, found her brother gunned and gotten a crease—the news services had a field day of it; TV, radio, papers. They even dug up all your past history; you'll be having people quizzing you again on how you got out of Nicaragua with General Ramirez's army beating the brush for you after you took his cat house apart in Managua. If you're smart enough, you'll drop it here and leave it—and the doll—alone. Otherwise, you'll be swimming the Mississippi in a concrete overcoat."

"Thanks for the tender sentiment. Your presentation was good, too, Don. Now. What do you know about the family and the situation?"

"About the family, nothin' but good. Rick had made his pile himself, the hard way. Bought a sunken tug boat on tick when he was a kid, raised it, and started barging on the river. Bought a couple more to finance himself in law school. Parlayed them into an ocean fleet finally, as the Harrison Steamship and Cargo Company. He dreamed up an auto-loading piggy-back system, and the unions dropped on him like a ton of lead. Know Bloody Maurey?"

"By reputation. That's Bloody Maurey Nacchi, isn't it? The hood that heads up the Dockside and Seaman's local?"

"The same. That's the boy you're spoiling to fight, old chum. When the unions tried to tie up his line and break his shipping system – it cost a pile of longshoreman jobs – Rick didn't have sense enough to say Uncle, but did know better than to try a frontal assault. He hired a couple of the biggest private agencies in the country, bought a couple of city detectives, and a newspaper man, and set them digging. He wanted not only heresay, but definative evidence against Nacchi and his whole tribe, and planned on breaking the union by jailing all of its top hoods. He was – I heard – prepared to present this package to the grand jury when he got back from his trip – he'd spent the couple of months sifting and correlating all of the reports, whipping them into courtroom shape – which, being a lawyer in his own right, means he must really have had the goods. The old boy didn't day-dream; he was a hardheaded realist who knew the score, and wouldn't overrate his own case."

"Looks like reason number two for the sinking. Another was the pile of ice his wife had aboard – close to two-hundred grand. Know anything about Grissolm?"

"Just by reputation, Jeff. Stunt man type – do anything for a buck – smash a ship or an airplane. Hints he fired factories and dumped cars to beat insurance companies. Big or little, depending on how broke at the time. Ladies man for sure – and picked expensive ones; seldom local talent or pros from anywhere. Drank a lot, but never talked out of turn."

"Union tie?"

"Hell, he was a seaman – which of them haven't?"

"I don't."

"You're not a seaman, anyhow. A damned seagoing snoop with enough money to loaf and an inclination towards suicide. An ambulistic accident looking for a place to happen."

"Don," I said sadly, "You've been reading that damned book of Webster's again. The descriptions are good, but the plot is lousy. I'm planning on locating and salvaging the VOLSTOK. Want to go fishing?"

"Yeah, damn you. I'm getting tired of this joint. But I don't want to—it's just that I'm too bored to resist."

"I'll have some local business. Give me a couple of days to wind it up. LOAFALONG's at the Marina on US 41 in Sarasota if you beat me down there. Oh—is Maurey still in the old hiring hall?"

"Yeah. But you're not going to...oh, hell—you're beyond reason. Give me a ring if you need a hand—or should I come along now?"

"I'll holler when, and if, Don. See you later." I tipped the glass a final time, strode from the bar onto Decatur Street.

Decatur, the street at the Mississippi River end of the Vieux Carre, New Orleans's colorful French Quarter, has none of the flavor or gayety for which the Quarter is world renown. An aggregation of chandleries, importers, and small company sales offices, the only bars are those drab holes filled with solitary drinkers—the flotsam of the world, who drop from merchant ships, drink up their pay, and go their way to some other dingy bar on the Decatur street of some other seaport town. Maurey's place was beyond the SIU hiring hall—in the next block of the ramshackle street. A dirty sign above the corner door of the four story building announced "Local 846, Dockside and Seaman's International." In small letters it added, "We do NOT checkerboard." I turned into a big central room filled with foldaway chairs, dirty spitoons, and a couple of battered library tables to which cheap pens were chained in testimony to the honesty of the brotherhood members. A barred window at one end was occupied by a harried little man with a green eyeshade; a couple of nondescript seamen lounged in chairs with newspapers over their faces, probably hoping for a call for work.

At the rear corner of the room a door marked 'Private' probably opened onto a stairway to the headquarter's offices. I entered and started climbing to the second floor which was barricaded by an unpainted plywood partition from access to the floors above. My footsteps resounded on the ancient planks as I passed doors marked 'Payroll', 'Public Relations', 'Women', and 'Office Manager'. A final door on the corridor read 'President. Private. By Appointment Only. Knock and Enter'. I ignored all but the 'enter'.

As I barged into the dingy office a plain jane type gal leapt from behind the desk – perhaps from the lap of the sleek little guy that occupied the swivel chair of green naugahyde and aluminum – a chair too rich for the building's blood.

Bloody Maurey Nacchi wore a gray gabardine suit, a greased-down hair do, and an expression combining elements of rage and fright. For a long minute the three of us were frozen in tableau; the girl was between a sitting and standing posture, crouched as though she couldn't decide when to leap, Maurey's hands were still half way around her. I simply stood, the arm with which I'd opened the door still raised.

Abruptly Maurey's right hand shot towards his desk drawer, with a leap I threw myself across the desk, slammed the center drawer on his hand, and chopped a quick, ineffectual blow to his face. He bellowed, struggled to free his trapped hand and to get out of the tilted back chair at once. The second blow was telling; his resistance ceased. I caught the right arm, extracted it, and with a free hand dragged out the Colt .45 for which he'd been searching. I thumbed down the safety latch, snapped back the hammer with my thumb.

Maurey's voice finally broke the silence—he held down the quaver with effort. "So what the hell now?" he demanded.

"You tell me, Maurey," I said.

"What do you mean, Mac? Who are you, anyway?"

"You don't know? I met you once at one of Bugsy's parties, chum. And again dockside when you were trying to sabotage a Greyban freighter. And later, in the same shindig, there was something about a cotton warehouse. Does that refresh your memory?"

"Tyler. Jeff Tyler. Yeah, you lousy bastard. So what?"

I swung a chop to his nose; it spurted. "No name calling, Maurey, pal and keep clear of those intercom buzzers," I added, noting his slowly inching hand with its big diamond solitaire.

"I'm an honest business man, Tyler. You can't come barging into my office like this. Who the hell do you think you are, anyhow? I'll have the police on you before you hit the bottom of the stairs."

"That'd be the safest bet for me. But I doubt it. What's an honest business man doing grabbing for a heater the minute someone walks into his office?"

"I thought you were...someone else. The door said private—you should have been announced. Or at least knocked. What would you think if someone crashed a party of yours like that?"

"Sure, an' you're the innocent type—got you nick-name contributing to the Campfire Girls every year. VOLSTOK II?" I expected a reaction with the fast tossed query, especially since I already had him off balance. But not the reaction I got. Maurey Necchi simply doubled up with laughter—honest, bellyshaking mirth.

"Tyler, you damned clown," he gurgled finally through his merriment, "get the hell out of here. I won't even sic the law on you, much less my boys. But don't come across with questions like that again — you're so far off-base you'll never get a sniff of it. Hell — why should I want to get to that one?"

"Because Harrison was preparing a case against you from a mass of data some eyes had dug out — and was going to the Grand Jury with it as fast as he got back. Because he was going to kill your whole lousy operation rather than back down on his piggy-back shipping and auto-loading plan."

"You're wrong I think." Maurey's eyes narrowed. "Dead wrong — and better drop it at that or the dead part'll be literal. I didn't have to go that route — I had the boy in my pocket already — it says here in fine print."

"Yeah? How?"

"My affair, Tyler. And it stays that way." I was puzzled — from where I stood, Maurey wasn't bluffing. Seemed to me the grand jury bit had come as a shock to him, and his musing seemed real. Regardless, I couldn't see a chance to punch his story now; he was too well composed.

"Okay, Maurey, we'll see. I figure on getting into the tub and finding out how and why it went down. If the stuff is there that I think I'll find, I'll take it to the jury myself." I dropped the hammer, snapped the safety catch on the automatic and slid it into my belt.

"My gun, Mac," Maurey noted.

"I'll send it to you — may need it to get by your goons in the hall. 'Bye for now, old chump." I stepped through the door, closed it behind me, and made my way unchallenged through the hiring hall. The man in the cage was staring my way as he stammered into the telephone — getting stomped I imagine, for letting me slip past. Tomorrow they'd put a bar on the stairwell door — or electric lock or something, I guessed.

I wasn't proud of my accomplishment — that of bearding one of the Crescent City's biggest hoods in his own lair. After all, I'd gained nothing but to remind him I was still around, still likely to create a nuisance — he'd had plenty to hate me for in the past. And maybe I'd tipped him to some dope he hadn't heard about before — that alone would make a big fly in my sticky ointment. Perhaps I could salvage something from the day; I'd check the insurance files and perhaps try to get some data from the police ident. group. Frowning with concentration, I headed for Canal Street and the impressive Laird's building.

*   *   *   *

I'd signed a salvage search contract with Gaylord, at the insurer's office so liberal and broad in authority that I could probably have gotten away with old man Laird's eyeteeth. "It's a license to steal," Gaylord had told me with a smile. "Gives you an idea how well regarded you are — but don't overdue it, Tyler." That's about all he could tell me. I'd already studied most of the company's data, and found little new in the New Orleans files.

Now I sat on a hardwood bench, with paint peeling, and carved with initials, outside a counter in the detective squad room of the NOLA PD. A girl with harlequin glasses, frames studded with rhinestones — the only thing fancy about her, leaned across the barrier. "He'll see you now," she told me, motioning to the swinging door section and pressing the button on the electric latch. I strode from the dingy front office to the dingy rear office, and extended my hand as Detective Sergeant Buckley, Homicide squad, rose from his squeaky chair.

"Tyler," he smiled. "Never expected you to come see me, willingly, Who'd you kill this time? And damned if you haven't got a pile of guts – writing in *my* name for personal and character reference on your application for a private-detective-license and gun-permit!"

"I was working in the job-description, so I thought I ought to have the sorority-card," I grinned. "Haven't killed anyone yet, but I've not even gotten my teeth into the affair, so if you'll give me a day or two, I may be able to oblige. Or I've got people wanting to kill me already, if that'll help."

I sat in the chair Buckley had indicated with a gesture. The graying, square-faced little man was sharp, was a fighter, and was one of the country's few incorruptible cops. Not that I'd ever seen him refuse an offer – it showed in the clear blue eyes – hard ones – and in the creases that furrowed his face. In the modest car he drove off-duty in a city where plenty of rookies could manage Cads. In a dozen ways.

"You asked me once to let the department help me out. I'm here to take you up on it," I told him, when we'd gotten cigarettes going. "I need it badly this time – I'm up against one I can't fight in the dark." Briefly I sketched the VOLSTOK sinking, my part in it, and my search through the talk with Maurey Nacchi.

"So you belled the old cat," Buckley exclaimed, his eyes dancing, when I'd finished the fairly straight account. "Boy, I'd like to have seen Bloody Maurey's face when you stuck his own gun in his teeth!" Buckley sobered, "Better watch it though – even if Maurey's not your man, he'll take a while to forget that stunt. He'll be out to get even somehow – hell, man, you even cost him face with his wench!"

"And probably for nothing," I admitted ruefully. "As

if things weren't already complicated enough."

"Do I detect a note of maturity in that admission?" Buckley asked, his eyes laughing harder still. "Last time we crossed swords you didn't seem worried about piling problem on problem." He blew a cloud of smoke ceilingward. "I don't know just what help I can offer at the moment. Your skipper—Chet Grissolm, has a brother in the Quarter—runs the "Golden Days," if I recall. Name of Clyde, I think. Clyde Durham—that's a family name; good old South stock, no less. I can give you the roster on Maurey's union—but it likely won't help you much..." he broke off and snapped some instructions into his intercom. "We'll see also if we have anything on Ippachio, as soon as the girl gets down with the files. You know, of course, that there's nothing official—"

"Hardly." I laughed, "You'd have the darndest jurisdictional dispute. Actually, no one knows how this stacks up yet. Grissolm was killed in Sarasota, but the killings that accompanied the sinking could be in English, International, or US waters—so it may take a battery of diplomats to iron the thing out in the long run."

"It doubtless will if you stay with it, Jeff. Even if it hadn't started out confused. There are still things about that BELL DEE affair that I'd like to know—officially the books are closed; part of the mob killed off each other, the rest got caught in a hurricane. Unofficially, things are just too pat. Did you know that Menotti had gotten the wreck's safe off the bottom and into his boat—but didn't have either diving gear or divers aboard? Or that a half-dozen engineers all worked equations indicating that the safe—even in a hurricane—couldn't have tipped with enough force to knock the deck and bottom out of his boat? And we assumed that a jurisdictional whinding in the mob made

Monetti gun a couple of his lieutenants out at the farm house—but he didn't do it with his gun; ballistics verified that when they recovered it with his boat."

"Strange," I said, with a mock-serious frown. "I thought the whole thing was sewed up and explained, from what you'd radioed at the time, and from the newspaper accounts."

"Someday we'll get together, and I'll go over the theory I've evolved. It works out beautifully—all the unknowns fall into perfect order. No loose ends. Yeah, the damned hoodlums deserved to get what they got—even if they shot each other it was a public service. But don't play God too often, Jeff. You're not immortal. And even people killing as a public service...are tried for murder when they're caught." He broke off as the girl with the harlequins walked in, dropped a pile of folders on his desk, looked questioningly until he shook his head, and left. He scanned the folders.

"Here's maybe something. Ippachio, Lorenzo— I'll jot the address and stuff as I go—wife works the quarter, chorus girl-and-prostitute, pro name Gia Gonzales. Longshoreman, one rap for looting warehouse, one for possession—heroin. No addiction record, so he was likely peddling. Both times the brotherhood shyster arranged his bond and defended him so he's above the regulars in the union—for the rank and file they hire one or another of half a dozen ambulance chasers. Could be you went to the right place after all, fella."

"Hope so. It's the only real lead I've got."

"You could just leave it to the police one place or another. Maybe search out the ship and salvage it like they pay you to do—or any other diver would."

"Don't even know where to start looking until I find out why she was bottomed. No one's told a useable story so far, Buckley."

"Okay. Union organization: President Bloody

Maurey Nacch, four aliases, conviction narcotics sale
1943 that kept him from fighting Japs. Conspiracy to
defraud, 1950 — key witness died in car accident, acquitted for lack of evidence. Ditto late fifty. He was organizing then, and had a rough row to hoe. '51, 2nd degree murder reduced to manslaughter, lack of evidence. '56 fraud in mail order real estate deal — selling
Florida swamps to pensioners sight unseen as building
lots. Acquitted — no proof of 'intent' according to the
second jury. The first was hung. Both had longshoremen in the ranks — though both had been 'suspended
for lack of dues payment a year before, and were quali-
fied as disinterested.' One of the jurymen on the second
round, Nicholas Lorraine, is Public Relations Manager for the brotherhood these days, at a substantial
salary." He paused for breath.

"Nice work if you can get it," I noted.

"His sister, Anna Marie is secretary to the president. Must be the doll you found in Maurey's lap, and
there's a Reginald Miles Logan, Secretary and Treasurer — how in hell did they pull a name like that out of
the hat? Oh — that second conspiracy deal on Maurey
— Logan and Lorraine were cited too; theft or misap-
propriation of union funds. And on the real estate
fraud — Maurey 'borrowed' from the union strike fund
to finance that operation. No record he ever paid it
back. God," he exclaimed, "it makes you sick! Those
poor devils breaking their backs on the wharves day
after day for peanuts, then Maurey and his hoodlums
take their earnings away from them. Partly in dues,
more for political action committees, more on loan-
sharking. And if anyone balks, or tries to get out, he
comes up floating in the harbor. Wouldn't help if they
got out, really; they don't know any other work and all
work assignments are handed out at the union hiring
hall — if a seaman on a ship looks cross-eyed at the cargo

they tie up the ship with a picketline, so all the jobs go out through Maurey, and anyone that bucks him goes hungry."

"Yeah. Another great example of the unions that are organized to 'help the working man.' One way to look at it; it's the same as a con game. The suckers join because they're basically dishonest—they think they can get something for nothing by letting the union extort it from their employers. Then when the shoe pinches, it's even too late to cry."

"Maybe you're a bit too harsh, Tyler. The good unions..."

"Hell, man, there are no good unions. Look at the basis: unions claim they have a commodity to sell, manpower. Do they? Of course not. If they sold labor, every union would submit its best man for each job, in the competitive market, and the employer would pick the merchandise he liked the best. Like honest manufacturers selling radios or cars. Manpower? Bull! The only commodity any union has to offer is violence or the threat of violence. Less work, more pay, or we bomb your factory or sink your ship!

"And the guys they're supposed to be for—what about them? They pay or they go jobless—worse yet, they die. Where I grew up the damned unions bombed ten houses in a two block stretch of Allen Avenue in two weeks time—killed and maimed women and kids mostly. Were they—the victims—the company management? Hell, no! They were workers who were competent, who were happy with their jobs, who had created their own job security by good, conscientious work —by the fact that they were needed—and who wanted no part of a 'voluntary' association pledged to get them more and more for less and less."

"Down, boy," Buckley laughed. "Okay, so I agree with you. But everyone from the Supreme Court down would be after my badge if I said so. *I* have to admit the *possibility* of a good union publicly; it gets to be such a habit I'm afraid to face the facts in private. Hell, Jeff, how long do you think I—or anyone in public life—would survive if we took your line on a soapbox?"

"Sure, Ted. I can see your viewpoint. And can see where a union—if not a simple extortion device, might serve some useful purpose. It could help its members to make more money—by conducting training classes in shop work, blueprint reading, industrial skills. It could improve working conditions—by financing and community building of—recreation facilities. It could manage a charity fund for its own needy. Could carry group insurance—paid out of the dues it raked in. It wouldn't have to be dedicated only to the proposition that with enough violence and threats it can extort its gains—can get something for nothing. That basic premise of the unions...is the basic premise of every thief who's ever lived. Sorry I launched a sermon —but I see red every time I hear the term 'good union' and speculate on what it's good for; on the premise on which it's built."

Buckley picked up the phone on the buzzer's third insistent ring, spoke a few gruff words, dropped the phone. "I'm sorry—emergency call; I'll have to break the visit short, but here's what notes I've jotted down and I'll have a steno transcribe anything else pertinent and have a car drop it off this evening."

"Hate to break the visit. Why don't you come by some evening? We'll shoot the bull over a highball—and I'll even listen to your theory."

"Good boy—it's a date. But will you agree with it if it's right?"

I shook my head with a sardonic grin. "Never— right or wrong. Or disagree." I stepped into the outer

office, Buckley swung past me, issuing instructions
as he rushed on through the office.

— — — — —

chapter

five

It was barely five o'clock, the earliest I'd even
thought about a session in the Vieux Carre in ages. But
maybe Grissolm — brother Clyde — would be keeping
shop by now. No harm in trying. I managed the Canal
Street going-home traffic in a couple of light changes,
something of a record, glanced at albums in the corner
Hi-fi shop, made a mental note of a new mood platter
I ought to try, and headed up Bourbon Street, the
Quarter's counterpiece.

There was little action in the night spots; that was
six or eight hours away, and the antique shops with
their glistening crystal candelabra from another more
gracious age, the Dalton figurines, and Spode china,
were closing for the night to let the bars have full
sway. An occasional combo made discordant sounds
as it tuned its instruments for the night's shows ahead,
here and there a juke box clammored, but the streets
and cages were nearly empty, semi-somnolent. A
sight-seeing tour salesman leaned against his bus, cap
pulled over his eyes, sleeping. Red, yellow, green tick-

ets, wilted by the humid day and hot sun were pinned to his sport coat lapels. I was tempted to stop at the Paramount for a steak, but my stomach rebelled at the thought. Not for another hour at least!

The Golden Days Cafe had been the Devil's Cave a couple of months ago, and something still different a couple of months before that. Only the grossest of criminality or mismanagement makes for name changing in the Quarter, this must be a really rough one, I decided. The building had once been a store of some sort — grocery, perhaps. Now the display windows carried a display indeed; their full height carried nearly full-sized photos of the strip artists in various stages of undress.

The girls were nearly life-height, and the photographer had hand-tinted them expertly with oils. A red and white aluminum portico awning extended over the street from the entrance doors, once glass lighted, but now plastered with smaller editions of the strip pictures that obliterated the windows. I pushed my way through the doors, found the cage brilliantly lighted. I started at the incandescence, then realized it was for the benefit of the cleanup crew still hard at work; by the time customers began flocking in, the dull — probably blue — indirect glows would conceal the age of the strippers, the cockroaches in the food, and the long settling cracks in the ceiling. Glamour they call the virtual darkness.

Finding a stool at the back end of the bar, I ordered a highball, and stared into the black eyes of a tall, good looking doll at the far end of the bar through the back mirror.

"Is the boss in?" I asked the barkeep as he shoved the glass across the bar and grabbed the twenty I'd dropped.

"Who wants to know?"

"I do. Friend of his brothers."

"What's his name?"

"Grissolm."

"Mr. Grissolm."

"I'm not working for him. Or asking favors."

"Mr. anyhow. And no. He ought to be around in a few minutes. Just went up the street."

"I'll wait." The bartender shrugged, wandered up the line to polish glasses. I noticed the girl again. Twenties probably. And stacked—if it was all hers. She ambled down the line, cigarette in hand.

"Gotcha' match?" she asked unoriginally, as she put an adequate posterior onto the complaining stool beside mine. I struck a match, held it for her. She blew it out. Again I tried, this time she held my hands to steady them, interlocking her left arm over mine to force my forearm hard against her breast. It felt like hers—Goodyear hasn't matched the real thing yet. Her lips were thin and hard, hair black, silky, and shoulder-length, and eyelashes real—not glued.

The bartender came down, put the drink she'd left behind in front of her. "I'd been going back," she lied, "but I don't suppose it matters."

"Sure it does, honey," I told her. "There's no customers up there."

Her eyes snapped. "What do you think I am, anyhow?" she demanded.

"A woman," I admitted. "And from appearances I'd put the price about mid-range."

"You bastard," she snarled. Then her voice softened.

"I suppose I shouldn't blame you, the way I just came up. But I really didn't have a light. And I didn't expect to meet up with insults."

"I'm sorry." It was my turn to lie—but what the hell —I had to wait regardless... "Can I buy you a drink to atone?"

"Well, I . . . I guess that's the least I can do. I'm drinking anisette. Are you a stranger in town?"

"No. And you're drinking out of my bottle if I'm buying. I don't pay for colored water."

"Now you're calling me a B girl," she snapped.

"Just letting you prove you aren't, baby. Do they whistle for you?"

"Mostly. Allright — your bottle."

"Two Old Taylor Highballs. Double 'em," I told the bartender. "And keep the bottle on the counter."

"You're a nice, nice guy. Did they wean you on roofing nails?"

"I wasn't a bottle baby. And I'm not weaned yet."

"Score one for you, I could get to like you a little, even. And my name's Gia."

"Gia Gonzales," I said. I said it, didn't ask. She turned to me, jaw dropping.

"You fuzz?" she demanded.

"Hell, no. Friend of the family. On your husband's side. But I just disowned him — don't like to chase friend's wives — even posthumously."

"What do you want with me?" she demanded.

"What makes you think I did? Hell, doll — you picked me up. Now I want what anyone wants with a good looking woman — you don't have to make a Federal case out of it."

"That straight?"

"Why shouldn't it be? I came down here to see Grissolm — but you're a hell of a lot prettier, I'll bet."

"You might like Clyde if you knew him," she giggled. "He's a real nice boy."

"That does it, wench. Can I buy you another drink somewhere else?"

"You name it. And also you name you — you're ahead of me thirty paces."

"Tyler. Jeff Tyler."

"Oh. You're the one that...I should have recognized you — the papers and televison. If you're ready, Jeff, let's hit the street."

The strain and tensions built through a grueling day dissipated as we drank, laughed, and hiked our way from spot to spot, watching the shows and listening to bands with beats as torrid as the sway of the stripper's hips. I'd tried to talk shop early in the evening, but given up. Her shrugging attitude and the infectious music brooked no sobriety.

Finally, in a cab we approached her duplex in an out of the way section of Jefferson Parrish — a side of the city I'd known little of. She lounged against me, head on my shoulder, rocking with the motion of the battered Plymouth on the worn pavement.

"Jeff," she said, straightening, "let's stop at the delicatessan next corner. I'll get us some steaks and stuff — you know, I really can cook."

"I know — you've had me simmering all evening, Gia."

"Flattery. But let's. And you can buy them — the guy that said the best things in life are free didn't know me. We can walk from the store — it's just the third block."

I shrugged, stopped the cab and paid off the driver, slammed the car door behind her. The cab gears ground as we turned towards the entrance to the neighborhood store — a grubby little building too obsolete for a face lifting, or even changeover to flourescent lights.

Glancing idly up the street at the disappearing tail lights of the cab, I stiffened. It swung into the next intersection, the driver apparently planning on turning into a through street half a dozen blocks ahead, to return to the Tulane thoroughofare and downtown. As it crossed the pedestrian stripe a truck — lightless and thundering — roared out of the side street. A diesel semi job – perhaps loaded – the juggernaut slammed into the side of the cab. Tires popped explosively, metal ground and screamed, glass spewed. The cab was hurled sideways ahead of the truck, then air hissed, the engine idled back, and the monster stopped docily, holding the remnant Plymouth jammed against a curb. I'd seen the cabbie silhouetted by a strategic streetlight at the moment of impact; had seen the limp flop of his head as his neck snapped.

Now I was dashing up the street, my companion forgotten, as the truck doors were flung open. The driver headed up the street, his helper jumped to the pavement, gun in hand as I approached. It had been obvious murder – the lights out, the truck geared down and fired up; I'd pulled Nacchi's Colt as I ran, thumbed back the hammer, and tripped the safety latch. I pumped a pair of shots at the man facing me, his gun dropped from nerveless hands, he fell without a sound. The driver was making headway; was far off before I levelled and triggered the gun. He staggered at the second shot – but could have stumbled.

Abruptly he threw himself to the ground, rolled under a parked car. A flame winked under it, a bullet struck the semi hood near me and whined into oblivion. I dropped – no point in even trying to hit him from so high an angle. Gingerly I crawled forward, between cab and tractor, then up under the cab's mutilated frame. A jagged piece of the tortured body ripped my leg. Ahead the gun flashed again; again the bullet added its bit to the wreckage about me. I took careful aim to the right of the flash location and fired. A fussilade replied.

People in the neighborhood flocked to windows and porches after the crash; one of them screamed a high wailing yell of pain that subsided into choked curses interspersed with sobs. If they had that much breath they weren't hurt too badly. I grinned through thin lips that felt parched. I couldn't have more than two – possibly three shots left – and only if the gun had been fully loaded.

I found a heavy hunk of headlight, pitched it grenade fashion from under the bumper. It hit on the sidewalk near my assailant; he replied with another burst of fire that marked him well. Beside me a tire exploded as I started triggering the forty-five; I felt the weight of the cab settle on me as I held my gun hand steady and fired until the hammer fell on an empty chamber.

There was a yell from under the car ahead, another shot, then a blooming flare of red. The car erupted, a yellow swirl staggering upwards higher and yet higher. A blast of searing heat flared across my face as I tried to pull in my arms to shield it, then the explosion shock-wave smashed me like a blow from a giant fist. The yellow wheeled through the color spectrum. To purple. To black.

"...had been punctured by the guy under the cab here," someone nearby was saying as I struggled back to consciousness. "And his last shot set off all the gasoline that was puring out of it. Imagine the bullets would have killed him anyway, but God, we'll need a bucket and shovel to get him to the morgue now."

"Joker down there's still alive. Get Danny to bring up a jack to get him out. Guess he killed the one beside the tractor too. But does anyone know? Was he in the taxi or what?"

"Grocer says he and a girl that lives around were coming into the store when he turned and went rushing up the street, shooting that horse gun. Says he don't know who he is – ain't seen him before."

Police, I decided, happily. With an empty gun and pinned under a car, I could get along without the trucker's pals. The crushing weight was easing; I realized that someone was jacking the car up. Abruptly I felt free, clawing the pavement I inched my way through glass and rubble. Hands on both sides helped me to my feet; someone wrenched the gun from my still locked fingers. I shook my head, identifed a police lieutenant and a pair of patrolmen. "Thanks," I said, weakly.

"Are you injured?" the lieutenant demanded.

"No. I don't think so. The car came down slowly, and the hoodlums missed," I added, and gave him the story, picking it up with seeing the lightless truck smash the cab—but neglecting that I'd just emerged from it.

He listened without interruption, turned, as I paused, to a patrolman. "Put cuffs on him," he ordered.

"Whoa," I demanded. "For what?"

"None of your goddam' business, Mac. If I say you'll go in a straight-jacket—you'll go." He caught my jacket lapel, jerked me forward, shoved back and jerked again, stopping his fist to smash into my chest with painful force.

Instinct took over; I no longer saw the braided uniform as I slammed a fist into his unprotected face, reversed a powerful jab into the plexus that doubled him for a smashing left to the nose that carried all of the rising rage and hatred of the moment. Cartilage snapped under my fist, blood spattered like water from a lawn sprinkler, the cop folded softly to the pavement. Belatedly the patrolman−unprepared for the display −grabbed my arms and twisted them in hammerlocks.

"What gives here?" a crisp voice behind me demanded. "For God's sake, Tyler!", it exclaimed. "Turn him loose men−he's only homicidal when the moon's full." I turned as the hammerlocks eased to face Buckley.

"Now, Tyler," he added, "let's see what you can do with this one to dodge charges of murder, assaulting officers, resisting arrest−and for all I know, attempted war and insurrection against the state of Louisiana. From the looks of the scene, you must have been using heavy artillery."

"Okay. First put the cuffs on this joker on the ground," I grinned, "so he won't interrupt. I want him charged with abuse of office, assault, and armed assault−I'll sign the complaint as soon as I get downtown." I explained the affair while the lieuteneant dragged himself to his feet and ministered his broken nose in a prowl car rear-view mirror.

"They're sure moving right along," Buckley mused, as I completed my narrative. "Just yesterday−no, day before−you found the raft; now they're after you with the biggest loads they can manage. The truck was stolen−that figures. Shame you managed to kill them both; we could have done with a little conversation."

"I'm sorry about the one that got away−wish I'd gotten him too."

"How do you figure?" Buckley was genuinely puzzled.

"Someone had to be across the intersection to finger the cab−they couldn't have seen it from the truck. Probably stood back against a building in the next block and waved them down with a flashlight. Come to think of it, it means a fourth — someone must have been following Gia and me around the quarter tonight to finger us to the guy that flagged the truck. Not too many gangs big enough to spread so thin — just one I can think of, I'd already figured for a spot in the plot."

"Poetic, yet!" Buckley's lips turned down depreciatingly. "And with Gia tonight — you sure don't waste time, Tyler. Where do you stand — anything new?"

"Just the wreckage you see around, Ted. Thought I might get somewhere with the girl ... "

"Yeah. I bet you did. But I was talking about sinkings. Look. I'll take the responsibility for releasing you on your own recognizance if you'll simmer down about charging the lieutenant — you couldn't win in the affair, but it's worth something to me not to see the force spit on unnecessarily."

"We could settle for an apology in writing. If your buddy's man enough to help he ought to be man enough to face up to an apology."

"I could let them take you in, and keep out of the case, fella. Come on. Be a sport regardless of what you're up against."

"Okay. But it's a favor to you — not the NOLA PD," I grinned at the wizened cop who answered with a slap on my mutilated shoulder. I said a round of goodbyes and so sorry's to cops and newshounds already flocking to the scene, dodged around a couple of blocks to get by the wreckage and crowds, and rapped finally on Gia's apartment door.

She swung the door open instantly; we both gasped. I, because of the change of clothes. Gia now wore a magenta negligee of filmy nylon, caught at the waist with long vees stretching both ways, but less revealing in nudity than wrap. Her coral tipped breast stretched creamily against the fabric, and her raven hair tumbled in disorder over the shoulders of the gown.

"Jeff! You're a mess," she finally understated. "Come on in...let's get you cleaned and bandaged." She fussed over me like an overprotective hen with a chick for a few minutes, sponging away dirt, rubbing merthiolate on cuts, snapping tape around gashes and greasing bruises.

"I didn't expect to wind up the evening playing nurse," she finally admitted with a rueful grin, "but it looks like you're better prepared to play patient than house, so I have to go along with the game. Do you tell me what happened out there—or do I have to get it from the newspapers tomorrow?" I went through the story again, tiredly.

"You have rough playmates, Jeff. Any idea who or why?"

"No. Was hoping you could help me out. Frankly I think Bloody Maurey had a hand in the caper, and I had wanted to quiz you about your ex—he was pretty well in with the crowd."

"That he was," Gia admitted. "And I'd never liked it—but expecially after Maurey figured ownership of Lorrie—that's what I called him—who could go Lorenzo?—gave him priority on 'lil 'ole me. I'd walked out on Lorrie several months ago—after he tried to convince me I ought to be buddier with his buddy. I mean —well, hell—you know what I am, but that doesn't mean I'm going to be pushed around like a goddam vegetable!"

"What kind of work did Lorrie do?" "Seaman?"

"No. He held a card in the union—had to be on their payroll for officers—but he never even took the ferry to Houma. Worked for Maurey all the time—odd jobs—keeping the herd in line—he was small, but rough, and whipped many a six-foot bale hustler on the docks when Maurey was organizing. He did the same with the shippers — batted a business agent around one day, or a scab or two another. Worked as a paid picket on strikes, drove sound trucks. I imagine he did a lot more that he never talked about. He never seemed to bright, but his books,..." she shuddered, "inorganic chemistry. Military explosives, pyrotechnics and chemical warfare, and a collection of stuff — mostly in suitcases — chemicals like chlorates. Diphenylchlorasine. That's a..."

"Tear gas," I finished for her. "Meanish type stuff that can hurt in overdoses."

"I know. He emptied our apartment one night — the whole building. But convinced everyone it was shot in through a window. Some joker mad at his organizing work, he said, trying to stop him. He was a halfway martyr for a couple of months."

"Still not much to go on," I noted.

"I think Lorrie was on his way out," Gia mused. "Those last few months. For one thing, he was as loyal to Maurey as a well-kicked spaniel, and I think Maurey is losing his grip. That smooth character — what's his name, Lorraine — and his snooty frau would like to take over. Think they'll make it sooner or later. And that oddball limey — Logan. No one's ever figured where he fits. Maybe he don't know himself."

"Did your husband know Grissolm? The skipper that bottomed the VOLSTOK?"

"Not so far as I know, Jeff. Grissolm was carrying a card in the union, so they may have met. I didn't get in on too much of what went on there — I didn't want to know, and they didn't trust me very far. Guess I just wasn't union-spirited enough. That was another deal. They wanted me to frame a bedroom scene with a guy that they were trying to organize — shipper — the Red and Black — a coastal steamship line. Not too big, but the old man was tough and respected on the waterfront. They figured if they whipped him into line a lot of other small operators he led would give up. His wife was a witch, so they didn't have much to worry about there — he checked into a Houston hotel to buy engine parts and they had a gal and photographer bull their way into his room as soon as room service found him undressed. You can figure the choice it left him — and he knew they'd whip him sooner or later. Think it was Lorraine's sister they finally cast in the roll — after I told them I'd do it only on the condition that I testify that I had."

Gia broke off to mix a couple of highballs; over the drinks our conversation merged into light nonsense. The frivolity wore on for an hour or so, finally, I called a cab, said an unwilling adieu accompanied by a promise to pick it up when the bruises healed, and gave the cabbie my address — with a silent prayer that he'd survive the trip.

— — — — —

chapter

six

After the third cup of coffee I still felt lousy. So I mixed the fourth half and half with Old Taylor and came out worse than ever. The papers gave me a lot of dope that I hadn't had — and didn't particularly want. The pair of hoodlums who'd swiped the truck and smashed the cab with it were little Mafia types with mile long records of misdemeanors and a few felony counts — narcotics possession and auto theft mostly. Both were members of the brotherhood and claimed longshoreman jobs to beat vagrancy raps from time to time. Neither employed at the time of the crime; one had worked a few days the month before. Both were suspected of peddling narcotics currently. So what? The data was copious — and completely worthless.

The cab driver had been Hammon Thomas, age thirty-eight. Married, three kids, and working a factory labor job as well as driving hack in an effort to make ends meet. No record — and none of the girl traffic almost standard with hackies in the city. A plain, nice guy. I felt lousier than ever; gulped a slug of raw whiskey — if ever my brand could be described as raw. Poor son of a gun, working like a dog, trying to be decent, getting rubbed in an effort by some damned goons to kill me. My fault, too, to some extent; I'd exposed him — unknowingly — by mere association. I'd roughed up Bloody Maurey, laughing at the certainty he'd try a comeback. I'd made him look like a bungling coward in front of his girl — had really condemned the driver myself. Sure, I'd had no idea where Maurey would strike or how — and had assumed all the risk myself. Yet... it hadn't been necessary — a smart-aleck stunt that had gained nothing for anyone, and had cost an innocent his life.

Yet I could still be on a tangent; it may not have been Maurey's work. Whatever, whoever, I vowed grimly — I'd get — it was all I could do now to atone. And the answers were on the bottom of some ocean.

I spread the section chart on the living room floor of my trailer, studied it at length. Finally I pencilled a light 'x' where Grissolm had been picked up, and 'o' where I'd found the raft. I entered by each the date of sighting, and approximate time. Finally I called the weather station at Moisant International Airport, jotted notes as I talked weather chart data for the past couple of weeks. Returning to the chart with notes, a volume of tide tables, and a parallel bar, I started plotting — trying to compute from wind and tide drifts the position of the VOLSTOK when she was destroyed.

The job was nearly hopeless; Grissolm had used sail and power on his boat, and I couldn't be sure I had the right date for the sinking. Finally I drew an ellipse on the chart; an ellipse discouragingly vast, one that covered a hundred square miles of Carribean Sea. But at least I'd narrowed my search to one ocean. Rolling the chart, I snapped a rubber band around it, threw it on the kitchen sink drainboard; I'd take it along when I went back to the LOAFALONG.

Running through the papers again — I'd checked only the front sheet — I found one useful bit. Sarasota P.D. had stamped 'closed' on their part of the case — the sinking was beyond Florida jurisdiction, they said, and they'd caught and killed Grissolm's killer. There was no reason to assume his death connected with the sinking of the VOLSTOK; it could have been a coincident, and his death simply the result of a long standing grudge on Ippacio's part — since both principals were dead no one could ever establish the details of the motive, they concluded. Convenient, I muttered. Real, genuine, morrocco bound convenient. And someone — Maurey? — had paid a big price for that convenience.

I phoned the LOAFALONG next, doubting that I'd raise any of my furloughed crew. The kid tender answered.

"You're up early, Old Master," the receiver acknowledged. "What's the emergency?"

I glanced at my watch, it read ten forty-five. "Have I threatened to fire you this week?" I demanded.

"No. And if you do you'd better do it right away or I'll file a grieveance with the Brotherhood Local," he warned in mock-serious tones. "Or didn't you know we were being organized?"

"Come again, kid. This is one area we don't joke about."

"No joke. Can't get on or off this worm eaten old tub without stumbling over the pickets. Signs say you're unfair to organized labor."

"They're right on that score. What's the occasion?"

"Like I said, we're permanent crew and carry tickets — they're having an organizing drive to get us all the union benefits — like my shutting down the air compressor when my eight hours are up and leaving you on the bottom until tomorrow. Also they want us to have union scale pay along with the benefits—but damned if I'm not tempted to forego the benefits; I can't stand the pay cut to scale rates."

"Thanks, kid."

"You'd better worry a little, though, Old Master. The damned grocery trucks won't cross the picket line, the fuel delivery man came by and left without putting a hose over. We're buying chow by the sackful and carrying it aboard under one arm while we shove pickets with the other."

"Have you tried the twelve-gauge?" I queried.

"According to the last NLRB ruling, it was unfair labor practice for an operator to threaten to 'shoot down pickets like a covey of ducks.' They enjoined him to stop threatening."

"I wasn't planning on threatening, kid. So it doesn't apply."

"That's what I was afraid of. Other things happening—they've a warrant out against you—for leaving the state as a material witness."

"They're crazy—they already have closed the case officially."

"Still a warrant. And for that matter, no one has told them you've left.—we said you expected to pick up some spare parts in Miami and we assumed that's where you are. Don Miller is aboard. Said you'd invited him to join the party."

"Yeah. Look, kid, things there sound rough—can you and Red hold the fort for another day or two?"

"We can hold the fort, Skipper, but we may have to handcuff Cookie to a stanchion—he—well, he has a sort of Gung-Ho attitude . . . last time he came aboard he pushed a couple of pickets out of the way—just elbowed them, sort of. One is still drying out and scraping bottom mud off his dungarees, and the other has light concussion. The damned union goons had their photographer on the scene — but Red told their lawyer he'd be laughed out of court if he showed photos of a sixty-seven year old beanpole whipping the heck out of a pair of brawny longshoremen. Red refused to even discuss the hospital emergency room bills."

"Tell Cookie he just earned a fifty buck bonus," I laughed — for the first time today.

"But there's more. When Cookie heard Red tell the Brotherhood lawyer he was an old beanpole, he tried to whip the mate, too."

"Sober, no doubt?"

"No doubt," the kid laughed. "As sober as a judge could be with a couple of fifths of hundred proof under his belt."

"Okay, kid. Looks as though you can hold it down. I'll be aboard as soon as possible — tomorrow or the next day. Have to talk to Laird's, police, and oddballs. See you soon." I dropped the phone, shrugging. When you step hard on toes you expect people to holler. Maybe I was getting somewhere after all!

*   *   *   *

"I don't know how to handle the thing," Lloyd Gaylord mused from behind his massive executive desk on Laird's Mahogany Row. The usual smile was gone, the athletic shoulders that required no jacket padding were slightly hunched. "I can't figure it, Jeff. That family was a big customer, and their influence will have a fairly lasting effect. I should — to impress our living customers — write that claim off as quickly as possible. Yet from another standpoint, how can I? A smaller amount, yes. And we'll cover the life and accident claims, regardless — already have that in the paper mill. But on the jewelry and the vessel... also there are ramifications bearing on double-indemnity payments."

"I can't advise you, Lloyd," I said. "From where I stand it appears that the skipper was paid to sink the vessel and kill the passengers. I doubt that he put it down in the slot — if so, there's no hope of salvage; the water there runs hundreds of fathoms, and we can't operate to any extent below two hundred-fifty feet or so. Granted it's possible to get further down than that, but working time even at two-hundred feet is a bare twenty minutes if you stretch it — and decompression time is fantastic. I think, though, that he tore her bottom out on a reef; if so, she'll be lying fairly shallow, and no where near the position he claimed. In that case — assuming we can find her, we'll be able to get whatever evidence is aboard. And the jewelry, for that matter. He didn't have it on his person when he was picked up, nor did they find it when they searched the dinghy, so if that's what he wanted, he planned on going back — or getting someone to go back after it. That could have been another reason for his giving a false position — he wouldn't have wanted anyone to beat him to the punch, and he'd have known he'd be watched for a while after the sinking."

"That could mean an organization too. No one without connections could dispose of gems of that size and worth. Actually, most professional jewel thieves never plan on selling their loot — they have an insurance company 'buy' it back by way of a 'reward' to some shady private dick that acts as intermediary. We know it, but the company has to make the best bargain they can — it's cheaper to pay the thieves fifty grand for a quarter million bucks worth of insured loot, than to pay off the claim and have the thieves, when they find they can't fence the stuff, toss it off a ferry boat and loose it forever."

"Of course, you're encouraging thievery by dealing knowingly with the thieves."

"I've listened to that argument. Preached it years ago myself, Jeff, but thieves would exist – and would steal – whatever you did. Some of the stones we carry policies on could never be replaced at any price – they're art objects in grinding and setting, and priceless rocks basically. Major diamonds – or gem finds generally – are even fewer, and a stone like the Cullinan for example, may happen only a couple of times in the world's history. We can't afford to have some scared sewer rat deep six a treasure like that – ignoring the cost in policy payoff; it would be criminal to have it lost to our culture. So we deal with the thieves through a thieving private eye. They get a pittance compared to the insurance we'd have to pay, and the gems come back to life again, which whether recut or discarded they wouldn't otherwise. The same thing – even to a greater degree – is true of paintings; they can't be recut; either way we pay the thieve's ransom – whatever it may be – or the world loses a Piccasso or Rembrandt to a goon's pen-knife."

"I'll say I agree – maybe. Teddy Roosevelt said it, 'Millions for defense; not one cent for tribute'."

"We pay a lot for defense. But when the defense fails, we bargain the best way we can for an uneasy peace. At any rate, that's the theory. In practice, what are your chances of finding the VOLSTOK?"

"I can't give you an honest answer yet, Lloyd. If she's in the area I think she'll have sunk in, there's a hundred square miles to search through. Can't see any way out but to hunt by plane – a boat would take forever. There's not a good chance – but perhaps a fair one – of finding her there. If she's anywhere else – patticularly in the deeps, it's hopeless."

"I appreciate the honesty. Discouraging, isn't it?

Could you give me a time limit—some idea of how long you could productively search?"

"A week or ten days once I'm on location and working. Another two or three to get organized. If I haven't found her by then, nothing but sheer luck will ever turn her up."

Gaylord's shoulders straightened abruptly. "Allright. I'll hold claims up to two weeks. Do whatever you can and keep me posted." He rose and extended his ham of a hand.

*   *   *   *

- - - - -

chapter

seven

My thoughts were disorganized as I piloted my big yellow Cadillac ragtop up Canal Street through the busy afternoon traffic. I'd stopped at Buckley's office after leaving the insurance building on the off chance that something new had developed. It hadn't — beyond Buckley's getting thoroughly stomped for releasing me, and for siding with me against the Jefferson Parish police division.

Jan Harrison had returned home, he'd told me, apparently well enough to get by with another couple of doctor's visits and a lot of rest. Also the Florida police had made inquiries based on their warrant, and had established that I was in the Crescent City. I turned automatically onto Gentilly Boulevard, threaded my way past the city pumping station, and finally swung onto Chef Menteur Highway, US 90 to Tallahassee.

The Harrison house was on Chef Highway; perhaps I should stop there on my way home. I'd accomplished nothing so far; had drawn a blank at every blind turn —

with a wry grin I speculated on handing in my recently acquired private detective's license — or perhaps taking a 'ten easy lesson' mail order course that *Argosy* so often advertised.

Jan's house was a revamped post Civil War job, magnificently restored to give an ante-bellum appearance, with broad arched front and latticed breezeway. The starkness of the white expanses was broken with stone planters, loaded with an array of caladiums, roses, and pointsettas, that splashed color from ground level to a six foot height, and the pillars of the breezeway anchored climbing roses with a profusion of scarlets and reds. The house and location spoke of close to a hundred thousand dollars at going prices; no surprise from what I'd heard of the family's economic and political affluence.

My Cad didn't shy from the hitching post at the edge of the long circular concrete driveway; the cars are reliable machines. I swung into the breezeway, made my way back to the front door, and banged a knocker with a lion's head as I stood between a pair of bronze mastiffs that guarded the entryway.

The maid who answered my knock was a crisply uniformed brunette in her thirties, attractive, but with her sex played down by the decor of her uniform and surroundings. She assured me that her charge could have no visitors, and that even an inquiry was futile; finally, however, she took my card and trudged up the circular stairway with ebony bannister.

I heard a door open and close, then a distant, muffled feminine voice shouting, "Jeff! Come on up here right away." I took the carpeted steps two at a time, followed the voice to the end of the hallway, and into a bedroom designed for giants. Easily twenty feet square the king-sized bed containing one small blonde was lost against a far wall amid a living-room full of black oriental-modern furniture. But better than what I'd seen before; tasteful, and expensive looking. I approached the bed. Jan, clad in white shorts and halter that showed an angry flush of crimson skin and burn peel between them, motioned the maid away, and extended a hand.

"Gee, it's good to see you, Jeff. And to feel like it, by the way. In the hospital I couldn't do much but feel half-way sore at you for saving me so I could go through the torture of burns, intravenous feeding, and so on."

"You look pretty chipper, now, Jan. Didn't expect they'd release you so soon, though."

"The famous Harrison temper," she grinned. "By the fourth or fifth tantrum they lived through they were glad to see me go – I guess I gave them a bad time from the minute I could raise my voice." She sobered. "Any new word on the sinking?" she inquired.

"No. I'm leaving for Sarasota tomorrow morning – think I'll drive down so I can take a car load of extra gear along. Expect to get under way soon after that to see if I can locate the boat and get down to her. From what I've been able to guess and calculate, I think I can find the boat – and that she'll be lying in shallow enough water for salvage."

"How on earth did you figure that? I'd have thought it would be impossible to even get an inkling. Gee, I wish I could go along as cabin boy, or mascot, or something. I – I'd like to be there if you find the VOLSTOK.

"You wouldn't really, Jan. It would simply stir up things that ought to die and be forgotten. And the LOAFALONG will probably sail without me – I plan on searching by air with my boat standing by in the neighborhood to hook over the wreck if and when I spot it from the plane. May have a couple of searchers out besides myself, for that matter, the insurance company's crowded for time and wants to get your claim — and the jeweler's settled — as soon as possible, so I'm running hard for time."

"That's right," Jan frowned, "Mother did have that jewelry aboard — she'd had it appraised by a Nassau Jeweler — an odd little Englishman named Tull, I think. Said he was the only one she'd trust, so she had to have him look the stuff over before she'd buy it. Silly, I thought, she deals with reputable houses, and after all, they're bound to be making a profit on whatever they sell. Say," she exclaimed, "do you suppose Chet sank the VOLSTOK to get that jewelry? There was a pendant diamond and a lot more — somewhere around a hundred, hundred-fifty thousand dollars worth, I imagine. Maybe that was the motive!"

"It could be, Jan. Laird's and I are working along that line. And also considering the union deal — the evidence your father had planned to give the grand jury when he got back would have been plenty of motive, too."

"Where on earth did you hear anything like that?" Jan demanded. "There's one that's news to me!"

"What?" It was my turn to be startled. "I understood that your father had been correlating evidence he'd gleaned from a couple of newspapers and detective agencies to give Maurey Nacchi — 'Bloody Maurey' — a hard way to go because of the interference he was getting on his ship auto-loading systems."

"It's news to me, Jeff. Dad did spend some time in his cabin working on papers and reports — but pertaining to his shipping, I think. This had been strictly a pleasure cruise — he'd been working like a dog for years, and he just let down and relaxed completely — I don't know when I'd ever seen him enjoy himself before, but he certainly wasn't doing much work on the trip."

"Must have been the jewels, then," I mused. "That narrows it — and also makes me look a little silly. I've taken Bloody Maurey for one fall on the thing already."

"I could be wrong, Jeff — but I don't think so. Dad would surely have talked about it if he'd been doing anything of the sort — he never kept business details a secret in the family; he talked shop a lot and even asked for advice ·once in a while — on things where he thought a female opinion was worth anything. Needless to say," she laughed, "there weren't many of those occasions." Jan dropped her head to the pillow, closed her eyes momentarily.

"I'm afraid I'm wearing you out, Jan," I said, "I'd better get along."

"I wish I could say no, Jeff, but I'm not in such good shape yet — the doctor's probably had better sense than I did. But," her eyes were pleading, "you will come back real soon, won't you? I — I owe you so much for saving me, and I want to say so much that I . . . I'm not ready for yet."

I caught her hand, "I'll be back, Jan," I promised. "But probably not until I've seen the VOLSTOK — it's my target for now." I rose, said a quick goodbye, and reaching the top of the stair, I vaulted astride the ebony bannister, taking the sweeping curve with increasing speed that nearly wrenched a exclamation from me. I hit bottom, staggered a couple of steps to catch my balance, and found myself confronted by a stare of astonished distaste frozen on the maid's proper face.

"Thank you," I told her courteously, as I let myself out the massive oak door.

*   *   *   *

I nosed the Cad into a parking slot near the French Market, snapped the switch off, pocketed the key, then remembered that it would soon be dark and stopped to lock the doors. Granted they could cut the top — and sometimes did on convertibles they thought worth looting, but it would increase the hazards a bit.

Crossing Decatur Street, I made my way back to the Golden Days Cafe, wondering as I walked whether Clyde Grissolm had heard the opera, or named the place at random. There was no one in the bar room as I entered; even the back bar was untended. A door at the rear read 'Rest Rooms', another beside it 'Private.' I took the private door, found it entered a store-room, with a second door on the opposite wall. Hand poised at the far door, I paused as a male voice spoke inside.

"They didn't manage, then," it said, nasally. "Look, it's too dangerous. After all, I'm his brother." There was a pause. "No," the voice insisted, "there's nothing yet. No one has even quizzed me — or acted like they knew I was alive, but I still can't stick my neck out. Besides, he has more lives than a cat.

"Hell, no!" it exclaimed after another pause. "Your boys were professionals and had everything in their favor — I'm not, and can't stick my neck out that far. Tyler's a brand of poison I won't take if I can help it."

"No, I'm not afraid of anything or anybody — you know damned well I'll take on anyone that comes up. If the price is right and I pick the battleground. On this one though, I'm vulnerable. Allright, I'll talk, but that's it, Nicky. You're wasting your time coming over. Yeah — goodbye." I heard the phone drop into its cradle and stepped, abruptly, into the little, paper-littered office, filled with a battered steno desk and chair.

Clyde Grissolm could have been a pug — sometime or other. He had the heavy build, the cauliflower ear — but he'd gone to seed. Paunchy and cherry-nosed, he didn't look formidable now as he stood in shirtsleeves, half-stooped over his desk on which a cigar was curling smoke in a butt filled ash tray. He looked up, startled, with hazy blue eyes that carried the fear he denied in their depths.

"Hi, Clyde," I said pleasantly. "Will this battleground do, or would you rather pick a neutral corner?"

"You're ... "

"Jeff Tyler. What did you tell Nickey old boy you weren't going to do to me without coaxing?"

"I—" he broke into a string of profanity, "you was listenin'," he finally accused.

"You're pretty dull, old buddy," I told him, smiling. "It took a long time for that to soak in. Now, give with the details—all I got was your end of the conversation."

"You ain't gettin' any more, Mack. Now get outta' my office before I call the cops. You're trespassing."

I slid the phone across the desk. "The number is ORleans 70000, Clyde. Ask for Buckley—he normally tries to find murderers after they kill, but he doesn't mind preventing one now and again. And there'll be one for him to handle in a few minutes. Yours or mine. Shall we see which as we go along?" Still smiling, I slid Maurey's forty-five out of my belt, thumbed back the hammer, snapped the safety latch on—just in case I got careless. "Or maybe Nicky, if he turns up real soon, and he seemed anxious, didn't he?"

"What do you want, anyway, Tyler?" Clyde's eyes bugged at me, his lips writhed.

"The whole story. Like why Nicky's pros were after me. Like who Nicky is. Like why he wanted you to do something about me that scared you so badly. Like what you know about why your brother scuttled the VOLSTOK."

With speed deceptive for his condition, Grissolm hurled a file spike. It grazed my shoulder, sticking painfully before it fell to the floor with a metallic twang. He smashed the bottom of the whiskey bottle on the edge of the desk, swiped at me with the razor-edged shard as I threw myself back across the office. "Didn't figure you to use the heater and bring the house down," he snarled as he hurled himself across the desk at me. He raised the bottle remnant and lunged; I sidestepped and smashed the heavy automatic barrel down on the outstretched wrist. He gasped, face contorted with pain. Stepping in, I lashed the gun across his face viciously. The cloudy eyes glazed, he toppled backwards, hit the floor with a look of sudden horror. He grunted — a grunt of mixed pain and surprise. The eyes rolled, the mouth worked hard to get words out. Foam formed, then the foam turned bloody as I watched, puzzled.

"Nicky Lorranie," he gasped. "Tried... truck... don't want you to get the stuff — not because...," worried, I stooped over him, saw the base of the paper spike, the spreading crimson stain on the back of his shirt. The bloody foam — a lung injury! "Jurry," he gasped finally, "get the doctor... memo book..." His eyes turned up into their sockets, his torso shook, then was still. I looked closely. He was alive — just fainted.

Glancing through his memos, I called the doctor I found listed, told him to bring a meat wagon with him and closed the office door behind me. There was a second door in the back wall of the storage room. I opened it into a corridor, lifted the bars on another door and found myself on a side street. I circled back to the front entrance, parked on a bar stool, and ordered an Old Taylor highball from the now dutiful bartender, sliding a ten across the counter as he set the iced glass down.

"Seen you before, ain't I?" he inquired.

"Yeah. Came in last night to see the boss, but he was out, so I took off with a gal that was loneing it at the bar."

"Oh yeah, I remember now."

"Boss in now?" I asked. "Still want to see him."

"Nah, he ain't. Night off. Try some other time."

"Okay. Thanks, anyway." I pocketed my change, killed the drink, and left as a bustling man with medical bag rushed by me in the entrance. In the distance a siren moaned. Perhaps the Brotherhood again, I wondered, as I idled down Bourbon Street. No, I decided finally, nothing could be gained there. I'd be as well off at home – where I could study the dossiers Buckley had sent me, if nothing more.

* * * *

– – – – –

chapter

eight

My trailer was at once spacious and compact; I reached from an upholstered chair to plug in an electric percolator on the kitchen drainboard, then grabbed the highball glass already prepared, kicked off my shoes, and shifted around for maximum comfort, and opened a *Newsweek* magazine. Later I'd snack at Gene's Diner, on the corner, but for now, a little rest and breathing time would take precedence over all.

Castro, I noticed, was boasting now about being a lifelong Commie. People should be surprised? With annoyance, I dropped the magazine at the second insistent tap on the door, struggled into the just discarded shoes and swung the door open.

"Come on in," I offered with a smile, noticing the diffidence of the woman and boy who fidgeted on the patio. They entered, the boy in his teens, I judged, straight, healthy looking, with black curly hair — deferred to the woman, an aging, sharp featured, thin one whose face registered a life of fighting adversity. His mother, I speculated. Not likely to be looking for a salvage diver. Probably a contribution to some whindig or another.

"I am Anya Strobel," the woman began with an accent—German, I decided—that overpowered the English completely, "Mr. Miller said that you we should come and see," she continued, the pace increasing, "about the schweinhunden und der ge—"

"Wait, Mother," the boy admonished with a grin that that broke the tension, "let me tell it. You get too excited." To me he added, "Not that I blame her—I can hardly talk about it myself."

"Sit down, folks," I offered. "I'll have some coffee ready in a minute, it's perking now. Then you can tell me vas ist lose mit der verdamter schweinhunden."

"My name is Harry, "the boy added, "Actually Heinrich, Jr., but Harry's easier in school. Do you understand German?"

"Not really. Word or two here or there." I poured a couple of cups of aromatic brew as the perc. shut off, passed it to the guests and returned to my highball. "You're welcome to Old Taylor," I suggested, "But I didn't think you'd accept an offer."

Harry shook his head. "Certainly not around mother, anyhow. And rarely, in any case. I don't want to take too much of your time, but Mr. Miller insisted we should come see you—he said some of our information might be of value and that you might...help us... not money..." he hastened to assure, a worried note in his voice.

"You mean Don Miller, I take it?"

"Yes. And he said you could be trusted. You see, he's done so much for us. Our community house, he built it, and coaches the basketball team."

I'll be infernally damned, I thought, with a wry

grin. The little gambler would cut out his tongue before he'd admit a charity like that. Aloud I commented, "Except with women. Go ahead, Harry, tell your story your way."

"I may. Did you read in the papers about the house being bombed in Jefferson Parish a couple of months ago?"

"No. I was at sea — don't follow news too closely on shipboard."

"Then you will want to see the papers." He extended a sheaf of clippings. "They will be faster than I could explain. It was our house."

I scanned the sheets, feeling a sweeping revulsion and horror at what these bombers had done. Fights — open, aboveboard ones can get rugged, wars were worse, but the sadistic fury of men who'll attack the unarmed, the defenseless, is yet more terrifying. The photos were graphic; the ravaged house, the sheet covered body on the police ambulance stretcher, its face covered.

"I'm sorry, Harry, Mrs. Strobel." You run out of words fast in circumstances like these.

"We are sorry to impose on you," Harry shrugged. "It is unfair to ask others to face having to offer sympathy. Yet, we were told that you wanted information on the Brotherhood? The local 846?"

"You bet I do!"

"It was they who bombed our house. Father had not joined them. He worked for a company in which the pay was good. One with a long waiting list of good men who were worthy of good jobs. The union had had organizing elections in the company — three of them — and had only a few men vote for organization each time. Finally they started to picket the company and terrify the employees into joining the Brotherhood — so they'd have to vote the right way at the next election. They got some — probably over half of them, beating them, threatening them, threatening their children. And they had their kids on us in school — fighting us, framing us in class for things they did, calling us scabs — and a lot worse. Father didn't join; he said he liked his job, he earned his pay, he got what he deserved, and was proud of it."

"He said he couldn't look himself in the mirror if he joined a union and fought the men who paid him every week; he'd be just a traitor. Not only to his employer, he said, but to his adopted country — America. He said that in America everyone should be free to sell whatever they could for the best price they could get — whether their crops or their product or their labor — and that no one should be forced to buy anything — including labor — at gunpoint."

"Your father was a great man, Harry. I hope you realize how great."

"I — I try to be like him. I fought them too," his tone was defiant, but proud, his jaw jutted. "No one's ever told me anything like you did before — I was the kid of a dirty scab, they said most often. Anyhow, a bunch of the guys believed in dad — believed what he said, and wouldn't join. It's a small company, they hadn't . . . the union . . . thought it worth bothering to organize before, but now they're getting ready for a nationwide strike to cut out auto-loading of all kinds, and to try to get lifetime employment contracts regardless of need — like those railroad telegraphers, I guess. It's stealing — just stealing — to make someone pay you for what you don't do — or what he doesn't need done."

"How old are you, Harry?" I asked, as he caught his breath.

"Almost sixteen."

"Hope to God you remember that when you're forty," I said.

"But I keep wasting your time. I'm sorry. What I wanted to say; Dad surprised them as they were setting the bomb on the porch – he tried to shoot some of them; he'd known they'd try something worse than they'd been doing. And one of them lost something out of his coat pocket – a card case with a driver's license and union card, as he ran away."

"Great scott! Didn't you tell the police?"

"I had picked it up before I – I fainted," he admitted, eyes downcast. "And put it in my pocket. It got lost when they took me to the hospital. Then I got back home and found it it the shrubbery. But the police had already quizzed me and hadn't believed me – said there was no reason at all to think the union was tied up in it – that it must have been some crazy firebug, so I knew better than to give it to them. I tried Mr. Casey – Jayne Casey, the special counsel for the Senate Rackets Committee – and he told me about the same thing. I told him about the card case, though. He was in town for a couple of weeks."

"Where the devil is it now," I interrupted impatiently, "You have it with you?"

The boy looked crestfallen, "No," he said ruefully. "I had heard Dad talk about Rick – that's Mr. Richard Harrison – and how he'd whip the union if anyone could. And I gave it to him before – before he left on his trip."

"Damn! Sorry," I added to his mother, "and when I could ice them down. Did you check through it, Harry? For God's sake, whose name was on it?"

"The name was Nicholas Lorraine on the license and union card. He's ... "

"I know who he is. Anything else in the case?"

"Just business cards – some realty company, and the union. The realty company was in Florida. I don't recall the city."

"East or West coast?"

"West. I looked for it on a map at the time. It was near Tampa."

"But you can't name the realty firm?"

"No." The boy drooped still more. "I wish I could do more for you, Mr. Tyler."

"Harry. You're a lifesaver. You've given me a gigantic break — you've damned well given me the whole story, I think, by the time I tie in the pieces I have already. I'll pay whatever you wish for the information." I could have bit my tongue, wishing I'd never said it as the boy's carriage straightened and his face turned crismson.

"I didn't ask for money — or come for it," he said, voice taut.

"Forgive me, I seldom meet a man nowadays." I extended a hand; he took it. "And," I added lamely, "I thought maybe your finances might be a bit strained at the moment."

"They may be," he replied crisply," but I don't beg or sell stories like a stoolie." He was still smarting from the insult. "I will be working soon. Dad had insurance. And a joint-checking account — that was frozen until any tax claims against it have been settled."

"Any job prospects?"

"No. But some people have told me to come back next week or so."

"Would you work for me? Starting immediately? No," I reversed myself, "it would be too dangerous."

"More than being bombed in bed? I am almost old enough for a work permit. And big and strong for my age. I want to work for you, Mr. Tyler — for whatever pay you find me worth."

"Have there been any attacks, any incidents, since the bombing, Harry?"

"Tonight. Twice the phone rang—once mother answered it, I got the second. There was no one on the line either time. Perhaps it's melodramatic—but that is why I decided to come to you. I had been afraid to trust anyone."

"You and your mother will stay at a motel tonight. There's one at the east end of this trailer park. I'll call the manager and make the arrangements as you leave. You will not return to your house until it's safe. You're on my payroll as of now, and I'll give you advance enough to buy whatever you and your mother will need for a couple of weeks. Meanwhile, you'll need a good night's sleep—you'll be driving to Florida with me in the morning."

I snapped off their gratitude; they made me feel foolish, waved them towards the motel office, and called the manager for accomodations to be charged to my account. As I dropped the phone it rang; I answered gruffly.

"It's Gia, for—Oh, God, hurry..." there was more—a sort of gurgle in the phone, a thud. I slipped my familiar .38 into my belt, jerked on the first jacket I saw to cover it; in moments the yellow Cad was charging across town with little regard for lights and speed signs.

*   *   *   *

The apartment lights were on; disdaining courtesies, I slammed the door open and charged in low, expecting a fusillade of bullets. There was nothing. Not a sound. I glanced around, jerked the gun out belatedly, walked towards the bedroom.

Gia Gonzales was sprawled on the floor, the phone receiver lying on the carpet besie her. Her torso was bare, with livid blisters breaking the cream of the skin on her shoulders and breasts. Cigarette burns! A half-slip was wrapped about her hips, and one slipper remained. Nothing more. There were welts across her back, more burns on her legs, thighs, and arms. Someone had enjoyed their work, I thought grimly. The room stank of burned flesh and hair. And cigar smoke.

She was alive, I realized, as my shock-numbed brain began to function. Her breathing was regular and sound; she'd simply fainted. I searched the closet, pulled out a suitcase and crammed clothes into it at random — how the hell would I know what a woman needs for a trip? I added some stuff from the bureau drawers, carried the suitcase to the car and tossed it into the back seat. She was more difficult. I lifted the limp body — deadweight is four times as heavy as the same amount of kicking, giggling girl on her way to a bedroom and pretending to struggle for her virtue.

Wrapping a robe around her was harder still — and the danged thing gapped all over the place when I was finished. Well, I decided, if the vice squad didn't nail me on the way, it'd give the hens in the trailer park one more to chortle about. I gathered her up. As her face fell against my shoulder, I caught a whiff of Choral Hydrate — the Mickey Finn of the Barbary Coast days. She'd be out a while yet. Finally she was in the car, propped against the door. I raised the top for what small cover it might provide, and drove back home. Drove carefully and slowly — I didn't want to explain her to some random cop that saw me miss a stop sign.

With effort I made it, straightened her as comfortably as possible on my bed, and rubbed the burns down with a patent remedy. Vasolene's best for bad ones — but this would offer some measure of relief for the pain she'd experience from a hundred little blisters when she came around.

Standing back, I looked for a long time at the ravaged body, caught in mixed feelings of mounting rage and temporary helplessness to act on it. I knew what story she'd tell when she regained consciousness — and added one more to the list of grievances I'd file with the Brotherhood soon. But it'll be a new grievance processing procedure for them, I vowed under my breath. I scratched a note and thumb-tacked it to the bedroom door in case she awoke confused without rousing me, pushed the door shut, and picked up the telephone. More things to do — and tomorrow an early departure.

Buckley was half-mad, half-puzzled, half-amused with my demand that he join me afloat. The bait I offered was too big; he decided to ask for unpaid leave if he couldn't convince the police commissioner he was traveling on official business. I broke the connection, dialed again. A sleepy voice answered. "Lorraine?" I demanded.

"Yeah. What in the bloomin' hell . . . "

"Tyler. I hope to kill you myself. If I fail, I'll leave it to Louisiana on the basis of the evidence on the VOLSTOK. Just thought you'd like to know." I dropped the phone, picked up the receiver again, and gave Bloody Maurey Nacchi the same message.

No. Gia wasn't a prude — nor do I wait for invitations generally. But who wants to sack up with a gal in her shape? I dropped off to sleep on the living room couch after sliding the .38 under a cushion.

_____

chapter

nine

I didn't get away by eight o'clock. Opening my eyes, I found Gia standing over me, shaking my shoulder gently. She was fully dressed, had coffee made and breakfast cooked. Only the pain and shock-induced creases at the corners of her eyes, and the involuntary wince as the cashmere sweater rubbed open a concealed blister were witness to her ordeal. The girl was beautiful . . . smart . . . and spunky as hell. I liked her.

Her story was no surprise. There'd been a knock; half expecting me, she'd opened the door to Lorraine and two goons who quizzed her — persuasively — as to what she had told me, and what more I might have known and confided in her. I was getting them scared, now — they'd show their hands more often. Lorraine. Public Relations Officer. Cigarette burns and nude women. Okay. My turn was coming.

Then the phone. Lloyd Gaylord.

"Did you know? Of course not, I haven't told you — " he began, his voice adding to the display of excitement in his grammar. "You may not have to salvage the

VOLSTOK'S cargo."

"What? Lloyd, it's too early in the morning for nonsense."

"No nonsense, Jeff. My Miami office — Redmond — was approached by a detective firm, if you could call it that, last night at home. Said he'd been contacted by a man who hadn't identified himself, but who wanted to negotiate for any 'reward' that might have been offered for the stones in question. The usual line — a straight-out bid from the thief to sell them back to us."

"It's a phony, Lloyd." My disgust registered in my voice; I wouldn't have expected him to be taken in so easily.

"I don't think so." Gaylord's tone was reflective — a cover for the fact that his mind was made up. "After all, the agency in question — Mike Storm's in Sarasota — has a reputation for, and history of, arranging jewel 'recovering'."

"A reputation for being a thief is a recommendation?" I queried. "If so, great world we live in."

"I explained it all the other day, Jeff. No use getting ouchy or moral about it. And yes — he's recovered stolen ice before. This means that he's probably telling as straight a story as he can under the circumstances this time; and that he wouldn't make an overture without some pretty good assurance that he could deliver."

"Or he's — on behalf of a really sharp operator — trying to keep me away from the VOLSTOK until it's too late to find anything on her."

"There is that, but then he'd have to negotiate with us anyhow."

"Not on that union evidence he wouldn't."

"I think you're barking up the wrong tree, there," Gaylord's voice was patronizing. "There's no real proof that such evidence ever existed — I'm convinced that the sinking was aimed at stealing the jewels, and that somehow they've been gotten ashore. Maybe hidden in the dinghy or in the outboard gas tank. Everything was searched, but the shake might have missed them, or they may have been gotten off first. At any rate, I think we may as well wait until we find out whether Storm can deliver before we launch an expensive search for the vessel —"

"I don't. Any my contract gives me authority to take such measures as I find in the best interests of my client. As you said, it's a license to steal. I'm going on with the search as quickly as possible."

"Don't be obsteperous, Tyler," Gaylord's voice hardened, the chiding, the friendly warmth gone. "All we're asking for is for you to delay your work until we determine whether it is required. We get along well; you work for us and we with you often. I have a great deal of regard for you personally. Don't make me talk about having our legal department break a contract when a few days will decide the issues."

"Go to hell, Lloyd." I slammed down the phone, cussed it as it rang again. A female voice this time. Janice Harrison. She asked about my health, my plans, was I still driving to Sarasota, wouldn't I reconsider and take her along — she wanted to at least be around the people avenging her family's death, even if she wouldn't be able to help much. She talked and I listened, my impatience growing as the minutes ticked by; finally, disconsolately, she surrendered and hung up.

Then Gene — did I want the ticket for Anya and Harry Strobel's lunch charged to me? I did.

My brother called, mumbling meaningless figures. I hadn't had the time to check the stock lists for six weeks. I brushed him off; told him to hold onto everything, buy nothing, and take a part-time job if my com-

missions were too small. I shouldn't have — the old duf-
fer meant well.

It was noon before I swung the big yellow Caddie
across the Industrial Canal bordering the vast Hig-
gins Boat Works. I held the accelerator down and drove
with an attention that left Harry and Gia white-
faced, tense, and silent. Poles and fast moving cars
fled away behind me, my normally seldom used horn
buffeted traffic to the edges of lanes with its imperious
demands. On lightly-trafficked straightaways, the big
job began to float — I'd never felt a Cad light on the road
before.

The truck and livestock-checking stations in Mississippi flashed by; small buildings with big parking lots
lined with waiting semi's. Gulfport and Biloxi joined
the kalideoscope of buildings, color and traffic. Somewhere I stopped for a tank of gas, I next stopped to pay
the toll for the tunnel under Mobile Bay. Despite the
power-steering and roadability of the car, my shoulders
and arms ached, my eyes were bleary as I swung onto
the coast highway with a straight shot Sarasota. I
couldn't make it — hadn't intended to — in a single
jump.

But as I swung into an ornate stuccoed motel, I
knew I'd gained the hours I'd lost, and could hit Sarasota and the LOAFALONG early enough to tool her
into sea before dark tomorrow.

It took only a few minutes to arrange for three rooms
— and the manager's dismay at my decision to put Gia
in a separate was hilarious. I sent Harry to the cafe
adjoining the office to eat, ordered for Gia and me from
room service, and dragged a bottle of bourbon from my
suitcase to pass the time until the food arrived.

The meager conversation on the trip had elicited
very little; I'd established that the Strobel kids —
the younger trio — had been taken to an aunt's for pro-

tection, that the name of the town on the business cards had something to do with fish — (Tarpon Springs, I wondered?) — and that Gia's rage against the brotherhood had flared even beyond the level induced by her torture when she'd heard Harry's story. I mixed the bonded whiskey with ice water, handed Gia a glass.

"Here's to crime," she said, raising it, "if that's what it takes to lick the Brotherhood."

"I can't understand it," I mused, as I sipped the potent water, "how the devil they get the control they do over their members; it isn't sensible that people should torture, murder, bomb — do anything on order like a bunch of trained seals."

"Jeff," she laughed, "don't tell me you don't know the facts of life at your age! You don't!" she added, noting the surprise on my face. "Allright, I'll give you the picture — and take it from me, I know. Bloody Maury is one of the public-spirited boys who's always working on rehabilitation projects, though most of his contact work is done through his smooth limey, Logan. That one can steal a billfold while making his victim cry with remorse over the plight of humankind. He's always on the lookout for new talent — has an in with parole boards in half a dozen states. When he finds a likely one, he has one or two companies that are trained bears — and have to be to keep from being strike-bound — offer the convicts jobs, since employment is a condition of parole as a rule. Then, when the cons report to work, they find that the companies are a closed-shop, they have to join the union to work. They go to the Brotherhood hall and find that there's an initiation fee of fifty to a hundred bucks — depending on the job. Since they're fresh out of stir, they're broke. So the treasurer — Logan again — offers to loan them a stake. At twenty-percent interest. After all, he says, a lot of guys jump jobs, they're poor credit risks, and so on. This isn't twenty-percent a year, Jeff, it's twenty-percent until payday.

"Then on payday, the company has deducted union dues, taxes, social security, ship's store charges, uniform costs, safety equipment, group insurance premiums—yeah, you guessed it; there's nothing left to pay off the initiation fee. So Logan's sympathetic—but openly suspicious. After all, he explains, he knows the man has been paid, and that he has a good job; he hates to look as though he's being harsh, and all that. So he'll let the loan rock along another pay period—at the same interest rate. You can figure it, Jeff. The hundred comes out to a hundred-twenty in two weeks, the next interest charge is on the total, so the second pay the poor sucker owes a hundred-forty plus. And again he has to let it ride, because of deductions and expenses. Or maybe the probation officer has hinted at a gift—that's pretty standard too. So pretty soon the guy who planned on going straight when he got out of stir is working off the bill for Maurey etal—first as a paid picket for four bucks a day—then on 'special assignments' that at least keep the interest in limits. Finally, seeing he has the backing of the union and its lawyers—also its paid politicians—he finds he can work on the dirty jobs full time and come out ahead. Meantime, what kind of picture has he gotten of society as a whole? A crooked employer who sold him into union bondage, a crooked probation officer that overlooks all the probation rules as long as the gifts keep coming in—a 'working man's' union that exploits its members and murders the workers who refuse its ministrations, and a bunch of cops and politicians who take pay to back the stinkin' play."

"For God's sake, Gia, if you've been sitting on information like that—"

"It's common knowledge," she said, "but it's hard to

get evidence — nearly impossible. All the victims have incriminated themselves — how can they testify? And to whom — the man they pick may be on the Brotherhood's payroll; if so, they'll be found floating in the river the next day or so."

"But there must be ways — "

"There are, or were, Jeff. I'd talked to Rick Harrison — spent a whole evening with him and his wife. And if he hadn't died, maybe he'd have been able to do something. I had hoped so, anyhow."

I opened the door as a rap interrupted; a waiter wheeled in a loaded tray, arranged the food on a table between a pair of upholstered chairs, took his tip, and backed out bowing ludicruously. Pretty hungry state in the off-season, I thought.

"It isn't always cons that they get to do their dirty work," Gia added as she attacked her sea-food plate and longingly surveyed my steak — women; they do the damndest things! "The people run an employment service too. When there's a job shortage — and that's pretty standard these days with shipping way down — they charge a few bucks a week for a longshoreman's job, twenty a month for a deckhand, and running on up to a hundred a month for a captain. No one has to pay — unless they want to work."

"I suppose they bill in advance?"

"Good boy. You're wising up. They collect in advance — and for the likely suckers, Logan's always around to offer his long green if they're short 'til payday."

"The more I hear, the happier I get," I muttered. "I wondered sometimes if I was wrong and the world in step. Now, I know."

"Have you ever wondered if you were right, Jeff?" Gia mused. "I sort of doubt it. You have so much assurance — a sort of hard core that nothing can touch. Sometimes I'm almost scared of you — and I know I wouldn't want to be on the other side."

I laughed. "Any good looking woman around can get to me; if Maurey really wanted to whip me, he could probably do it with you."

"I'd like to think I could mean that much, Jeff. But there's no point in your kidding me, or me myself." She swallowed the final scallop, tipped up the inch or two in her glass. "I wouldn't have been surprised if you had ordered your steak raw. Yet you're the first guy in ages that's treated me like a human being. Separate rooms, yet," she grinned, "and thanks—even if it's only because you don't like to stare at blistered hides."

Our waiter cleared away the wreckage of the meal, and Gia snuggled into my arms on the couch, our drinks fresh, and the television turned to a news program. It added nothing to my store of data; I'd hoped for anything at all bearing on the Brotherhood of the VOLSTOK. Finally Gia rose, pulled me erect, and threw her body into mine.

Afraid of tearing blisters, I held her gently at the start of the kiss, but as her demanding lips and tongue quested, my grip grew harder. I bent her back and forced her body into conformance with my own. Finally she broke away gasping.

"Guess I've said goodnight, Jeff," she said softly. Turning, she rushed through the door. Moments later I heard the door of the adjoining cabin open and close, shortly after, the hiss of a shower. Well, I'd asked for it, I grinned wryly, as I pulled off my clothes and dropped into the lonely bed.

_ _ _ _ _

chapter

ten

_ _ _ _ _

A nightcap makes me sleep more lightly than normal; several, lighter still. What wakened me, if anything, wasn't important. There I was, though, wide awake, all my senses focused, trying desperately to gather in some elusive threat. The full moon lighted the motel courtyard, shone in the windows in long rays with nearly the clarity of sunlight. The front window of the cabin was open a couple of inches; *the front window of the cabin was open a couple of inches!* I'd left it closed! I inched my head up — someone was working around the window — stuffing it with rags, I decided. Gingerly I felt around, located my thirty-eight as I watched his furtive progress.

There could be two or three of them. I'd so far, located only the one at the window. He'd apparently finished his job, I heard a guarded footstep in the garage port between the cabins. Quickly I swung out of bed, slid into slacks and shirt, opened the back window. The screen was an aluminum tension-latched job; it unhooked in moments. As I dropped to the grassy slope behind the motel, I heard the throaty growl of my Cad engine starting. It was equi-distant around the long stretch of cabins — either arond the front and past the office, or around the back — either way I had to cover nearly half the drive completely exposed. As I started for the rear, I stumbled over a stepladder stored with rolls of roofing, a few cans of tar, and sundry paint gear. I tried for silence as I nestled the ladder against the low shed type roof; the gentle scrap was probably covered by my running engine.

Inside the garage, I heard the hood being raised, the tick of the engine accelerated to a gentle purr as some-one advanced the idle-set screw on the carburetor. By now I was on the roof, gun in hand, inching my way towards the edge. I still could see no one; with luck, the man tampering with my car was working alone. I stuck my head and shoulders over the edge of the roof and waited.

The hood dropped with a gentle clang; my quarry stepped from the darkness of the garage to pause just below me, looking around to assure the clear escape route. Deciding quickly, I smashed the long steel barrel down on his head; he crumbled soundlessly to the ground. Springing down, I noted the vacuum sweeper hose from my car exhaust to the front window; it figured. I caught the limp form, dragged him into the cabin, and lashed his hands temporarily behind him with his shoelaces — there was rope and tape in the car; but I didn't want to risk his recovery.

Out of deference to the accumulating gas in the cabin, I opened the doors and windows, shut off the car engine — cussing his jumper-wire that had to be disconnected before I could, accumulated bonds from the car, and made his bindings more secure. He was stirring and moaning as I began a search of his pockets, armpits, and belt.

These local 846 boys got around, I decided, as I surveyed his union card and driver's license. The name meant nothing to me; one of the flunkies, I imagined, kept in reserve for occasional dirty jobs. He carried a thirty-two calibre automatic—an Austrian job, fancily nickel plated, with imitation pearl handles. And an ugly switch-blade knife with five or six inches of honed-steel on call. Piling the hoard on a coffee-table, I lighted a cigarette, turned back to find his pain-and-hate-filled eyes boring into my back.

"Hello," I greeted cheerily. "I suppose you aren't going to start right off and tell me all about it?" He answered with a profane snarl. "All right," I shrugged. "I know most of the answers, Bud. I don't need you. And it seems a shame to waste all your preparations—I'll just close up and start my car again."

Closing the front door, I cranked the windows down, slid on a sport jacket to conceal my revolver, and dropped his automatic and knife carelessly into the pockets. Fishing through my slacks I found a key ring, selected a gold key with a Cadillac crest, and exited through the garage door. I started the engine in legal fashion, noting that I'd have to back off the idle before I could drive the car again, pulled the lethal hose off my tailpipe, then re-entered the cabin cubicle, gathered my suitcases, and started for the door again. "You ain't," the hood gasped. "You can't do this!"

"Sure I can," I assured him, pausing briefly. "You jokers get away with murder—and everything else—not because you have enough brains to keep you overnight—but because you count on your victims being disarmed by their own standards. You depend on legal-arrest, a fair-trial, and honest-witnesses, and on your victims playing by their own rules while you ignore them all. I'm playing the game your way, though—I caught you, arrested you, tried you, found you guilty, gave you a chance to make a dying statement, and am carrying out the execution. See how easy it is when someone takes you on by your rules?"

Lifting the suitcases again, I turned. "Bye now," I said, "the air's getting pretty thick in here."

"Wait. Wait, Tyler," the hoodlum gasped. "I'll tell you anything you want."

"Nothing I want—I know the answers—all I asked for was confirmation."

"Evidence. I can give you evidence—tell you where to get records—you can have it all. Don't kill me!"

I dropped the suitcases. "I'll get a typewriter—you can dictate to me and sign the copies."

"But the gas—I'm choking already."

"You'll last a few minutes yet. I'll leave a door open to stretch it out." I left, rummaged through my car trunk, returned with a Remington portable and perched it on the coffee table. "You can start at the beginning," I told the hoodlum. "And I'll type as long as the story sounds straight. The minute I smell a curve I'll close up house and walk in the park for a while."

"What happens after you've got it?"

"That depends on how well I like it. I might leave you with the exhaust, might turn you over to the local law—and possibly'll decide to turn you loose entirely. Let's go, now—I don't like the smell in here."

"I ought'ta hold out for a bargain—"

"You've heard the only one I'll offer," I snapped.

"Hell. I got out of Buford Prison—that's in Georgia— the rock quarry—in three years of a five year sentence for possession; they'd nailed me with a nice little stock of Horse. Affiliated Shippers and Drydocks were supposed to have a work contract on me covering two years probation, and the Brotherhood had paid my transportation to New Orleans through Traveler's Aid—who didn't have any idea what the score was. They were innocent bystanders. When I got in and reported for the job, they nailed me with a hundred-buck's initiation fee, and told me the transportation was a loan. And I had to have work clothes, hand tools, and odds and ends. Safety shoes, too. Then a cop from the 'Crime Prevention Bureau' hit me to register as a parolee and undesirable immigrant to the city, and wanted twenty-five bucks to keep from running me out of town. I found out later that there was no such bureau—actually—it was a racket setup by a couple of rookie cops that were too new to get in on the better grafts."

"Name the cops," I demanded.

"You're going to get me killed one way or another," he moaned. But he complied. "All in all, I was in hock to the union—through Logan, the treasurer, for about two bills and a half by the time it was all wound up. And he nicked me twenty-percent interest—said it wouldn't be fair to risk the members' funds on a con without a high return rate. That was 'till payday, by the way. Payday the union nicked me for a fine—said I'd worked over the legal overtime limit, and nailed a twenty-five buck can to my tail—and most of my check was eaten up be deductions. To spare the details, in seven weeks the union was into me for eleven hundred dollars, with a continuing forty-percent a month compound interest. And I got laid off—work contract or no."

"Logan squeezed down hard, then. He wanted hired pickets for a secondary boycott—and I walked the line twelve hours a day for four bucks, and six off the bill. I made a couple of bonuses, too—cracking heads when people crossed the line. Fifty a head, they wrote off. Which didn't even write off the interest, but it helped. They liked what I did with a club, though, and sent me

to special classes, finally — classes on strike organiza-
tions, picket line setup, factory sabotage, and explosives handling. Including bomb making. Held the
classes — 'seminars' — they called them, in an old War
II hull in ASD's shipyard. That's the real Brotherhood
office — all their important records, explosives, supplies,
are stored there. They've a couple of safes, file cabinets,
the ship's armory — all heavily locked, and they keep
their own guard aboard, while the shipyard's security
police also add to the defenses. Almost foolproof. They
can flood the old hulk any time they throw a switch."

"What year did this begin?" I interrupted.

" '56, about July fifteenth, I reported."

"And the set up is still the same?"

"Yeah. I was aboard night before last — for briefing
on this job."

"You bomb the Strobel house a couple of months
back?"

"No. Iggy did that — and some of the others. He got
killed in the truck they tried to get you with. You've
got them scared. After that, they're beginning to think
you're supernatural or something."

"Did Maurey order the VOLSTOK sunk?"

As when I talked to him, I was puzzled by the re-
sponse to the question, the hoodlum bellowed with
merriment. "He didn't know nothin' about it," he
finally responded.

"Why — who in the hell runs the Brotherhood anyway?"

"Maurey thinks he does. But he'll know better sooner
or later. Lorraine and his society bitch run it — and
they'll knock Maurey off sooner or later."

His report rambled on. Finally, convinced I'd bled
him of everything useful, I slid the papers over for his
signature, checked it against that on his union card. I
folded a set and slid them into a jacket pocket, stuffed

the originals into an envelope, addressed it to myself
care of Detective-Sergeant Ted Buckley, NOLA PD,
and sealed the envelope. There was a stamp in my
billfold, and a post box in front of the motel office. I
mailed the data before returning to unlash the little
hood. .

"One copy of your statement has been mailed," I
told him. "To me, care of an honest cop. If anything
happens to me, you're dead. The second copy will go
to Maurey Nacchi if you ever try to go back to work for
him. You could kill me for the third − if you have the
guts and luck; it's still in my pocket."

"But what can I do?"

"I'm going to get Maurey − and everyone around him.
You have twenty-four hours. I'll promise you that, but
no more. Do whatever you wish with it. Starting right
now."

The hoodlum didn't wait for another invitation − he
left like a three year mare from the starting gates. I
switched off the Cad, coiled the hose and stuffed it into
the trunk, pulled the rags out of the window, and
tidied up generally. It was nearly time to get up. Without bothering to undress again, I dropped onto the bed
and went to sleep.

*   *   *   *   *

The name was in the phone book, so I dialed while a
station attendant gassed and serviced my car in the
outskirts of Tarpon Springs. The town in one of Florida's older cities, long the center of the nation's sponge
diving industry, and the colorful Greek divers and
boat operators still congregate at a community pier
when in port. The narrow twisting streets, many shell
and souvenir shops in the old buildings of original
Florida archtecture, make the town one of the State's

most interesting. A pleasant feminine hello broke through my speculations.

"Mr. Casey in?" I inquired.

"No, he isn't," she replied. "He's down at the office, I think. That's on the Trail just at the south edge of town. Can I take a message?"

"No, thank you. I'll be dropping by the office soon; I'll catch him there." I added a goodbye and dropped the phone.

"Find him?" Gia asked as I slid back of the wheel.

"Yes. He's listed in the directory. Someone – wife I suppose – said he was at the office. South edge of town. Right on our way; we'll drop in for a chat. Or I will."

"Let's all go," Harry said. "I need to stretch my legs and I haven't done anything at all since you hired me."

"It's feast or famine in my operation, Harry. Relax, soak up the sun, and be glad things are peaceful at the moment."

"By the way, Jeff," Gia muttered, "I still don't believe that you slept all night in your clothes. What on earth were you up to? When I woke up you acted as if you'd just gotten to sleep."

"Just plain old laziness. I always sleep like a log. Watch for Casey's office, will you? We've mysteries enough without you inventing more." The traffic was heavy; momentarily I'd have swapped the big ragtop for a Volswagon as I dodged, inched and expected a crunch of fenders at every traffic funnel. Gia and I spotted my objective simultaneously; I swung into the curb, shut off the engine, and surveyed the building across the street. It was a fairly old three-story brick with display windows on the ground floor, and entry door centered between them. The left hand display windows carried the legend: 'Casey and Company, Realtors.' The right-hand window read: 'R. Miles Logan Construction Company. We Build On Your Lot.

NO DOWN PAYMENT.'

Glancing at the floors above, I read: 'Able, Jett and Strump, Attorneys' in gold letters across the narrow windows on the second floor while the third floor split the offices into smaller increments: 'Mike Storm, Private Investigations,' and 'Brotherhood of Dockside and Seamen, Local 244, Tarpon Springs.' All the eggs in one basket, I grinned, this meant that someone on the Rackets Committee — besides Casey — had a first hand knowledge of the rackets they talked about. I glanced back. Traffic was distant enough, I swung open the door and dodged across the street.

Inside, the building gave every indication of its legitimacy; a clean and neat office shared by a realty firm and a contractor. An attractive receptionist glanced up from her typewriter on Casey's side.

"May I help you, Sir?" she asked pleasantly.

"Shopping," I grinned back. "Do you have brochures on tracts or building lots?"

"We surely do. Would you like a waterfront lot or are you interested in inland lots or acreage? Or perhaps something along the inland lakes?"

"Waterfront, I think — I prefer salt water fishing."

She sorted through brochures. "We guarantee all of our lots to be dry and useable, Sir. No swamp, no hidden charges. And the prices listed are actual — there is no interest. We can furnish title insurance too — and any paid-up lot is so well valued that you can have a contractor — whomever you wish, of course — build on it without further down payment than a mortgage on the lot. Mr. Logan, for example — " she gestured across the aisle, "builds on such terms. You're welcome to any of his brochures, too, though there's no one in for him right now."

"Thanks so much," I said, mulling through the house plans and sketches, and picking up a couple of his cards. "I'll be by again when I make up my mind." With a smile, I left, turned the corner, and ascended the stairs to the third floor. The legend on Storm's door said 'Enter'; I did.

A gorilla sat behind a desk too small for him. Easily my height, the man was preactically as wide, his sport shirt revealing arms covered by matted black hair that also filled the vee of the turned-back collar. He needed a shave – and looked as though he always had. His hair was a black curly matt except for a glaring bald spot on the back of his head.

"Mr. Storm?" I asked.

"Yeah," he practically snarled, baring yellow fangs. "Who's askin'?"

"Me. Do you have facilities for making an investigation?"

"S'wat I gotta' office for."

"I want someone to check out a rumor that a private eye put the nip on a mess of ice off the VOLSTOCK II," I explained.

Storm's expression didn't change. His posture remained frozen, his breathing even, but a red glow suffused the vee of chest, the stub of neck, then flooded over the man's face. He moved with a precision incredible for such a hulk; one moment he was at the desk, the next he towered over me, blocking even my peripheral vision on the sides. He mouthed a stream of profanity, but kept his hands at his sides – apparently sure I couldn't elude them if he wanted to restrain me.

"Talk, Mac," he demanded.

"I said it," I said.

"Who the hell are you, and what's with the VOLSTOK?"

"Tyler. Under contract to salvage it. And wanting to know what kind of lead you've got on the ice – if you have one – it was stolen; I have the only salvage authority."

"When crooks get an agency to negotiate with an insurer, the stuff's always stolen," Storm told me. "We all know it—so what the hell? It's a fee for the agency, a recovery for the insurer, and a pile of boodle for the thieves. Now, what's your angle?"

"Just trying to confirm whether or not the stuff's aboard—whether or not your lead is reliable."

"Crooks don't stick their necks out to make jokes—of course it's reliable."

"Okay. Thanks." I turned towards the door; an arm snaked out and pinned my shoulder. "Turn loose, bud," I warned.

"There's a friend of mine wants to talk to you," he muttered. "I'll call him—"

The guy was probably a pro-boxer or wrestler—he couldn't manage the bulk so perfectly otherwise. So he'd be immune to ordinary attack; I could break both fists on his jaw without hurting him, I imagined. He outweighed me easily by eighty pounds; there was only one avenue open. My leg swung out and up with all the force I could manage; he moaned and doubled, releasing me. I slammed the knee into his jaw, almost at my waist level. Collapsing on the floor, he shouted profanity and called for help as I closed the door behind me, and dropped a hand into a jacket pocket. The door across the hall burst open—the union Brotherhood office entrance—and two men rushed into the hall.

"Tyler!" someone shouted.

"Get him," from another quarter.

The man nearest me flicked a switchblade from his hip pocket; a second was drawing a gun; I heard feet pounding in the hallways and offices as Storm's yells crescendoed. I triggered a shot at the ceiling light; it flashed brilliantly and darkened the hall. The knife-wielder lunged; I turned and let him slip past, clubbing him with the automatic as he went. Someone tripped over him as he fell. A gun crashed throwing bullets aimlessly. Storm's office door burst open.

"Save a hunk of him for me," he raged, as he stomped over the huddle on the floor. I was on the landing now; men were coming up, but uncertain of the fight or target.

"He's up there," I told a couple as they rushed past. "And with a gun," I added. I made the second floor, dodged into the law offices as more men hit the stairs. There was shooting on the floor above. I leapt back into the hall and dashed towards the street exit.

"There he is!" Storm shouted behind me somewhere. "Leggo me you crazy bustid!" Bullets splattered plaster near me, white powder flaked through the air. I leapt through the door and into the street, trying to get the automatic on safe and concealed from curious passers-by as I fled towards the Cad. I dodged through the traffic again, leapt into the car, and shot it into traffic, half expecting a following fusilade.

"Sounded drastic," Gia gasped. "I—doggone I was scared."

"Just converstion," I told her. "I asked a question, and they answered it. Sure will be peaceful on ship-board, Gia. I'm getting tired on this drive."

*   *   *   *   *   *

Fighting nothing but traffic, I finally got through downtown Sarasota and swung into the boatyard. The LOAFALONG was tied where I'd left her, adorned with a streamer of sign-bearing pickets proclaiming graph-ically that I was unfair to organized labor. Well ... I had no argument there. One picket leaned against the hull just under the wheelhouse; the others milled along the pier from bow to stern. I walked across to the leaner. "You're leaning on my boat, buddy," I told him.

He gave me a long insolent stare, lighted a cigarette, flicked the match against the leg of my slacks. I grabbed him by the shirt front, spun him away and hit him ineffectually as he staggered. Following up, I got in a solid one that sent blood spurting from his nose. He bellowed with pain as a couple of his fellows reversed their signs, club-fashion, and crouching, moved in. I feinted at one, he dodged as I spun, caught the club of the other and jerked him towards me, throwing out a foot to trip him into a hard fall as he passed. Across the lot, Gia screamed; I threw myself to the ground as a shotgun blast peppered the sides of the boat. My automatic snaked out; as I looked for a target, Red's voice bellowed a command to halt. I rose, approached the picket with the shotgun who stood frozen in the sight of my mate's carbine. Wrestling the gun from his grasp, I hurled it into the muddy channel, drove my gun barrel into his mouth and turned away as he fell.

"This is warning for all of you," I announced to the remaining pickets, "not to lay a hand on my property or anyone connected with it. I'm offering a hundred dollar bonus to any man on my crew who nails one of you while touching my boat." I held the car door for Gia and Harry, led them to the gangway and onto the LOAFALONG's crisp buff deck. The picket line was silent.

"Boy! I'm glad to see you, Skipper. Everything's up in the air here, really need you to untie the mess."

"Back on shipboard where it's nice and quiet?" Gia reminded me. I grinned wryly.

"Red Price, Gia Gonzales and Harry Strobel," I began. "Harry's crew for the time being, Red. Have the Pollack find him a bunk and get his gear straightened out. Better have Cookie whip up chow for us, too; we've been moving too fast today to even think about eating it."

"Will do, Skipper. Meantime, there's things – Redmon's aboard, for one – pacing the lounge, waiting for you."

"Okay. Settle Miss Gonzales in my stateroom, and come on up to the lounge. I'll get with Redmond. Gia, I'll see you in a few minutes; Cookie will have lunch by then." I turned, and headed for new problems. Redmond had been pacing, allright; the slight man looked like a prowling tiger as I strode into the lounge and offered a hand. He glanced at it, decided, and took it.

"Glad you finally got here, Tyler. We – Gaylord in New Orleans and I have been trying to reach you ever since just after he talked to you by phone. I – I'd rather you could have gotten the information from him, but I'm with Laird's too, and someone had to get stuck with it: our legal department has decided that your contract can be held invalid – and they are prepared to do so if you maintain your cavalier position."

"That's the opinion of your legal department – not the decision of a court of jurisdiction," I grinned.

"True, but they do not often err. As Mr. Gaylord had told you, all this is unnecessary. We need hardly place ourselves in such a strained relationship – "

"It's by your choice; not mine, Redmond. I know that the salvage rights components of the contract are cancellable only by my non-performance. If I delayed on the basis of your legal opinions, I'd be jeopardizing that portion of the contract by failure to perform, even if at your request, unless the request were formalized into a contract addenda."

"You have a point, Mr. Tyler. We probably could so amend your contract."

"But I won't enter a request for amendment. I expect to initiate my search immediately."

"Then you'll do it not with the aid of Laird's, but in

spite of us. We are convinced that the jewelry has been removed already."

I walked to the typewriter desk at the end of the bar, thumbed a couple of sheets and carbon into the machine, and banged heavily on it for several minutes while Redmond fidgeted. Red entered while I worked; he mixed a pair of highballs, shrugging at the shake of Redmond's head to his offer, and handed one to me. I gulped at it as I snatched the sheets from the carriage, handed one to Redmond.

"Here's your release from all finanical responsibilities under the contract," I told him. "I'll sign it with Red as witness. All remaining obligation will be maintenance of my salvage perogatives, to be conducted at my expense, without incurring any preliminary, facto, or post-facto obligation for remuneration for your company." I took back the copy, scratched my name boldly across the bottom, handed it to Red to read. He signed as angrily, stuffed the paper back into the agent's startled hand. "Now, if you'll leave, Mr. Redmond," I suggested quietly, "we have work to do." Red caught his arm, guided him firmly out the hatch.

Ted Buckley passed Redmond in the hatchway; the the detective was really prepared for a seaborne vacation, with white flannel slacks and Hawaiian-print sport-shirt replacing the usual low-keyed business suit. He grinned a little self-consciously and shoved the crisp new yachting cap back on his greying hair.

"One thing, Ted," I admonished, "never put on one of those caps until you've run it through the bilges, towed it on a fish line for a couple of hours and jumped up and down on it a few times – new ones have no character."

"I'll try that, Jeff – might make me feel more confortable, too – I've been in blue-serge so long I feel idiotic dressed like this."

"Come on to chow for now," I suggested, "and we'll try to do something about the lid later in the day." He and Red followed my gesture towards the dining room.

Introductions had been completed all round by the time we reached the table, Cookie had managed a seat on Gia's right, my kid tender — I'd have to fire that kid someday — sat at her left, and the silent Pollack was monopolizing the conversation, telling the aggregation of some of my more stupendous blunders. Harry started as I arrived, apparently expecting a break in the conversation — he didn't know how little respect I commanded yet.

"How," Gia demanded gaily, and obviously prompted, "did you ever manage to get out of Nicauragua?"

"Alive," I admitted. "Let's put it on a serious note, gang," I added. "We've time enough to get out of the channel before dark — and had better."

"Without fuel or supplies?" Red demanded.

"Have the orders sent out again after lunch. Tell them they won't have to cross a picket line — and I'll guarantee payment for all delays and damages incurred. We'll fuel and supply, then get the LOAFA-LONG under way — I want her in open water by nightfall. I'll organize an air-search to start in the morning, and will fly a seaplane looking over the search area while you're cruising into the sector in question — I know about where to look, I think. If we can spot the VOLSTOK by air, we'll mark it with dye and I'll have the plane land and transfer me aboard to handle the salvage operation. I'll give you the search-sector after chow, and remind me to take a CB transceiver along on the plane — it'll keep our chatter off the regular marine bands." I stuffed some more food into my mouth.

"Why don't you give us a break and stay with the air-search, Old Master?" the kid inquired. "We could get along real well without you. And even get some work done."

"Sorry to leave you with this wolf-pack, Gia. Maybe you'd be safer with me."

"Maybe, from what I've seen so far," she agreed gaily. "But I think I'll have more fun with the wolf-pack. Or are you jealous, Skipper?"

"No. I could fire them all and hire a bunch of old men — or maybe not," I added, noticing Cookie's fascinated stare.

"Go ahead!" Gia laughed," if they're all dolls like Cookie." She caught my hand. "At least you take it well, Jeff."

We bantered on through the meal, then I showed Red my calculations and scored a rectangle on his section chart. He nodded. "Think you're right," he growled.

While he phoned suppliers, I went to the marina office and — with a little dickering — bought it, completing the transaction as a pair of fuel trucks swung in and stopped short of the line of menacing pickets. Picking up my office phone, I called the city police. They debated — but had to act; grudgingly they sent out cars enough to haul away the pickets, charging them with trespassing on my personal property. We loaded fuel and supplies through the next hours; by the time the Brotherhood's attorneys had untangled the riddle, and the hall managed a new string of pickets, the trucks were departing empty.

A little later I sold the marina back to its original owner — at a three-hundred dollar loss.

— — — — —

chapter

eleven

The little Cub — a J3 Piper with an oversized engine, clipped wings, and Edo floats, seemed a bit puny as we skimmed over miles of open ocean. But an airplane was a plane — and a single engine is as good as a twin — as long as it runs. If not, there was always my boat within a few wet hours.

The pilot's name, stature, and temper matched: Short. And short of talk. He'd been knocking down a pile of money dusting the newly planted crops in the Homestead area. I'd hit it wrong: planes and pilots were scarce and expensive at the moment. The job had finally appealed to him — along with triple pay and a thousand buck bonus for success; so here I was.

I'd folded down the enclosure, but still the heat was intense as we flew, making a course straight out to the shallows and reefs that marked the southern limits of the passage from the Gulf of Mexico around the Florida Penninsula and Keys. The reef was not well defined; a succession of shallows stretching from a point near Key West through to the islands of the Bahamas, with a fork jutting past Andros and extending deep into the Carribean sea. Much of the water was passable — but it was territory for seamen, not novices, and many vessels, large and small, had crashed fatally into barely-submerged shoals and coral-heads throughout the area.

The sky was azure and nearly cloudless, the crystalline water below matched the sky in hue, and a blazing sun showed the ocean bottom through the surface of the sea. It was white sand in places, ranging as it deepened through pink sand to tan mud; coral reefs stood out starkly with whitecapped surfs over the shallowest. Back and forth we flew, up and down, as Short — not short on skill in flying and navigating, followed precisely the rectangular grids of the search-course I'd laid out for him at the airport. We'd returned once already today for fuel, dipping our wings at the LOAFA-LONG as it cruised easily towards the search-sector.

A flock of cruising gulls split to let our noisy bird through its loose formation, craning their necks to stare back at us with distaste as we passed. I was glad they'd given way — the impact of a bird that large on our prop would have meant a swim — anywhere else, would have plummeted through the fabric cover and smashed the underlying structure. Then, in isolated cases, bird damage has caused crashes. I assumed Short's ejaculation to be profane; above the engine it couldn't be heard.

Ahead the water showed white behind a speeding cabin cruiser; I shook the stick to draw the pilot's attention and pointed. Short nodded, the engine howl dropped to a staccatto buzz; the little plane dropped into a smooth, fast glide. We swept low across the water, a little to the right of the boat. She was making time — a good eighteen or twenty knots, with twin streams boiling from the screws. Dangerous pace for this water—I studied the boat and wondered. Possibly forty-five or fifty-foot factory job—Owens from the lines. Sleek and newish, probably not over a couple of years old. There was none of the normal yachting inactivity; bikini-clad girls lying on deck, or trunk-clad men with highball glasses and fishing tackle. This baby was here for a purpose, I decided—and more likely than not, the purpose matched my own! The engine crescendoed as Short pulled the Cub skyward, leveled at five-hundred feet, and dropped back into the search pattern, leaving the Owens to vanish into the sparkling distance.

A rising breeze kicked up a small sea as we cruised onward; tide shift increased it as the day progressed and the lowering sun edge-lighted the sea, cutting visibility through the waves. I watched the changes with growing disgust; if this got worse, we'd have to drop the search for the day. On the horizon, Andros Island appeared; now the sea was speckled with the little sand and coral islets—mostly unhabitable—that crowd the Carribean. Long jagged reef lines underscored the waves that broke whitely over them. A black shape rolled under the water and spouted a thin water stream; a Jew Fish—and far South for the time of year.

Abruptly I shook the stick; Short released his grip, and I kicked the plane into a tight turn, looking down over the low wing with concentration. Water was breaking along a reef—but there was one spot—at the center of my turn—where the reef-edged froth formed a rectangular pattern instead of a long gently curving line typical of the rest of the reef edge. I leveled, cut back the throttle, turned again towards the spot as our altitude dropped. Crossing at a hundred feet or so, I looked again; beneath the boiling surf was the outline of a boat! I wagged the controls back to Short; he held altitude in a vertical turn as I fixed my attention on the wreck. She was big — a cruiser obviously from her almost upturned bottom; I caught a glimpse of bronzed screws and rudders through a break in the surf.

"That the one?" Short shouted.

"Could be," I replied as loudly, "looks like it, but I can't say. Drop a bit, I'll look closer."

"Don't want my wingtips wet," he retorted, but the little ship dived shallowly to flare as the waves reached desperately for it. Again we passed the wreck; I'd bet on it now -- the superstructure, square and classic in design, the flared bow and high foredeck.

"Home, James," I shouted. "Drop me aboard." The engine surged, the little plane fought itself skyward, turning gently towards the Florida coast.

"No dye?" Short queried.

"No. Make it too easy for that Owens — she could beat me to it as is." I snapped on the CB radio I'd brought, leaned out the enclosure to give its antenna a chance.

"Red," I called, ignoring call-letter rules.

"On," the headphone crackled.

"Position sector-eight. Block nine-three."

"Roger."

"Make for it Red, I'll meet you."

"Roger."

I snapped the set off. There'd be no chance for triangulating on that brief a call -- by the FCC or the Brotherhood people. Distantly on the horizon I saw the Owens; she'd wind up in the ballpark if she didn't find the wreck, from the course she was making. Or maybe she'd hit the reef tonight and feed her Brotherhood crew to the fish. I could hope.

My impatience mounted as the minutes ticked by. Finally the LOAFALONG rose on the horizon, coasting towards us on her column of creamy wake.

"Land wherever you want," I shouted to Short.

"She'll come close enough for me to swim across."

He shook his head as he shouted a reply. "Too rough now – can't land."

"I have to get down – what the heck do we have a floatplane for?"

"Not for that –" he pointed at the cresting swells, now wind-shipped by the stiff afternoon breeze.

"I'll pay for the damned airplane."

"No, Tyler. I haven't washed one out yet – this won't be the first – pay or not."

"Short! I have to get aboard my boat."

"You're sitting on a parachute," he said laconically. I caught my breath; even the idea left me weak. Parachute? Hell when I'd been taking lessons I looked down every time I poised a plane for a spin and wondered whether I'd have guts enough to use one if the wing fell off! Until I decided I wouldn't. Suddenly I realized he was circling my boat in a lazy climg.

"We've got to land," I shouted.

"You, maybe. Me, no. So if you want to go. Go!"

There was no arguing, no gain. Short's mind was made up. Either I took the chute down or landed at Miami, recalled the LOAFALONG to pick me up, and let the Owens beat me to the VOLSTOK; for I was sure that it was their destination. I stared out the enclosure; a wave of terror gripped me as I thought of the downward plunge. Through my vertigo sky and sea blurred into a mass of writhing blue and green, for a moment I couldn't distinguish up and down. I pulled myself together, breathing shallowly against tightened diaphragm and ribs.

Somehow I unbuckled the safety belt, swung my feet out of the enclosure. The prop-blast caught them, twisting my knees painfully back against the steel fuselage structure. I couldn't do it! Whatever the cost, whatever the loss, I couldn't jump!

Briefly I felt a mass — a flying boot against the small of my back — a thrust. My ears were torn by a scream that rent the air around me as I was catapulted into the dancing blue with its zig-zag sun streaks of gold. I felt myself tumbling, felt a hand ripping at my shirt and belt.

'I've been kicked out of better places than that,' I thought, inanely. There was a rifle shot sound above me, the webs about me snatched me upright and to a stop. I stared upwards at a billowing canopy of white, clean and sparkling in the sun. My eyes cleared; I was drifting   slowly — almost   comfortably — downwards towards the LOAFALONG,which swept in a wide circle, awaiting my arrival. The Cub flashed by; a grinning Short waving through the still gaping enclosure opening as he wheeled towards his airport and dinner.

There was something I was supposed to remember about water landings in a parachute. Something I'd learned ten-fifteen years ago, I guessed. Oh — unsnap the shroud clips a little before contact and swim underwater if necessary to get out from under the collapsed canopy. And get shoes off and webs ready to strip if you couldn't swim dressed. I could. As the sea reached upwards for me, I caught the shoulder clips, snapped them loose. A familiar brine closed congenially around my face; here I was at home!

For a long moment I relaxed completely, sinking slowly in the tepid tropical sea, savoring and enjoying the bouyancy and comfort. Finally I stroked back to the surface to tread as the big white hull glided towards me, as the Pollack and mate threw over a boarding ladder and guided me aboard.

The kid handed me a bottle of Old Taylor. I gulped a long swig hungrily. "Nice of you to drop in, Old Master," he said. "Was it bad? Hard to get up nerve enough to jump?"

"Had to get aboard and that was the only way," I said. "Short couldn't land as rough as the sea had gotten. No. I just made up my mind and jumped," I lied, feeling abruptly again the weight of a flying boot in the small of my back.

"Who in hell was screaming up there?" Red asked, deadpan.

"Must have startled Short when I went so abruptly," I snapped.

Turning towards the wheelhouse, I walked away with dignity, hoping Cookie had something hot on the fire. Besides my girl.

— — — —

chapter

twelve

The sea had moderated with nightfall, the wind died, and the Carribean had become the place travel-agency salesmen spin dreams about. We coasted through a translucent sea under a thick black sky studded with a low hanging candelabra of brilliant stars. Our wake boiled the bright green of a witch's broth behind the transom, and the bow waves flashed like sparklers as the more brilliantly flourescent plankton sparked brightly enough to illumine the sides of the clean hull. With running lights extinguished, we ghosted along; as a precaution, I'd doubled watches.

The Pollack had the helm, with Harry Strobel, who was beginning to get his sea-legs, on bow watch while Red and Cookie alternated between stern and engine room. The kid was asleep—I'd need a tender—and perhaps, a spare diver—tomorrow. Gia hadn't made the sea-legs; she was moaning in my bunk as Ted Buckley and I lounged on the flying bridge within easy reach of the flaming stars just above us.

"A night like this could just about make me turn in my badge and sign on with you, Jeff," Buckley muttered contentedly. "I've never seen a sky like this — or a sea at night, for that matter. Many of these and I could almost understand you."

"Understand me?" I laughed.

"And why especially a guy like you — like you had been — wound up where you did. Oh, don't get me wrong; I'm not trying to preach any more. It would be futile, and you're not so bad anyhow, I suppose. But I still haven't ever figured you — why a top engineer just walked out — with the country — all the industry everywhere — screaming for engineers — and turned to a life like this. Sure, you make money — sort of. At least you have a pile of it stashed. But dammit — "

"Why does a guy walk out on a job most people would give their eye-teeth for?" I finished for him. "Why does he surrender the respect and prestige of a top job, the security of regular hours and a big company with insurance, retirement, and all — to get his hands dirty, to whore around, and to be regarded as maybe a borderline crook — or at least, shady operator and unwholesome character?"

"You said it better than I could have. And more brutally, Jeff. That's about it — I've worried about it from the night I first ran into you — "

"Half-naked with a nude girl dead in the bedroom of her apartment. Yeah. I remember," I grinned, remembering.

"So do I. We really shook you down — and when I saw the list — your degrees, books and technical papers, I was flabbergasted. It's so out of character. And I don't believe — never have — in people being out of character."

"That's an odd idea for a modern cop — you're supposed to think a tiger can change its stripes at will."

"I ain't a modern cop, Jeff. What was it, J. Edgar Hoover said about the 'cream-puff school of penology'? – No, I don't go for much of what it proposes."

"Look, Ted. Was I respected when I was in the factories? Hell no! I couldn't walk into the john without some snide cracks from the hoodlums about my being one of the wheels that sat with his feet on the desk and sopped up the money the working-men made for him. And speaking of money, the working-men make, did you ever wonder what was a fair pay for a working-man?"

"Well –" Buckley speculated, "I never stopped to consider. I reckon not quite what they always get."

"A fair day's pay for them," I snapped, "is what they can make in a day with nothing but their own two grimy damned hands. Nothing more. Anything else they make – whatever – they make because I or some-one like me gave it to them. A worker in a factory earns high wages because of the *machines* his *employer* has supplied for him – machines that multiply his earning power a million-fold; that take him from his own hand's capabilities and permit him to make parts by the hundreds and thousands – and to get paid accordingly. No one who has designed a machine, or devised a process, or invented a whole new concept of automation or production, has ever received a fraction of the worth of his invention – a fraction of its worth to the society to which he gives it. The punch press that raises the worker's output from ten-horseshoes to five-hundred car-fenders a day – and his pay from forty-cents to twenty-dollars – got personally very little from his invention but the satisfaction of having solved a difficult problem in mechanics. Edison, received for his invention of the light bulb nothing at all compared to the benefits reaped by society as a whole from his invention. I could go on and on – and often do," I laughed, "but that's part of the story. The guy who sits with his feet on the desk — and in so doing makes it possible for the working-man to work — has always been reviled, castigated — and frequently slaughtered or at any rate sacrificed economically to the instatiable greed of the workers. Society has never been — I say *never* — exploited by the rich, by the trained, by the competent. Rather, the reverse: the rich, the competent, the inventors, scientists, businessmen — have always been exploited by society. I got tired of being the sucker in the bit, Ted. I worked four or five months of the year for the looters — and the taxes it took me that long to earn paid for bigger unions, more giveaways to the beggars and incompetents, more power for the politicians who did the looting. Five months out of my life every year mounted fast as the years went by. Why should I have to sacrifice months yearly of the only life I have to support projects I feel are destroying society?"

"Put that way I guess you make sense."

"I simply quit — I needed that five months worse than the Lower Slobbovians needed the money they wrested from me. I bought a boat — figured I might make a half-way living with it as well as enjoying it — hell, I'd been a Frogman, and a boat-lover all my life — and if I didn't make a living, I knew I could go a few years on my savings and book royalties regardless. I *hadn't wanted to make money;* at least not more than the minimum on which I could escape paying taxes to forces and programs that were subverting the freedom of the nation — and, to a point, the world."

"But even here you haven't been able to escape success, Jeff. Even here, your ingenuity, curiosity, and ambition have kept you in a high bracket."

"I know," my grin was rueful. "But there have been compenstaions. I escape part of it; I'm not beleagured in the washrooms, and I'm not contributing added-productivity-potential to the guys who sue for a new contract every year to produce less for more pay. Most of my recent contributions to society have been the occasional scandal stories our buddy Thornton prints under his high-priced byline."

"Okay, Jeff," Buckley said wearily, "I can understand now — and I should have before. I suppose some of these thoughts have occurred to me — and I've read Ayn Rand too. But I can't agree — some one has to keep trying to hold things together."

"And the harder they try; the more they pillory themselves into greater efforts — the more they assure their own destruction. And destruction of the society they're trying to save. Remember the horse's motto in Orwell's ANIMAL FARM? 'I must work harder'. Until they hauled him to the hackers. Until they hauled him to the hackers... and their whole card house fell around their heads because he was gone!"

"I know." He sighed with resignation. "And I can't give you an answer, Jeff. Not even a good argument." We smoked in silence for long minutes, watching the spindrift fleck from the bow wave and spill back into the langorous sea.

"I wish I could," Buckley finally added, "because then I'd have an answer for myself."

I dropped a hand to the square shoulder of the aging policeman. "I'll hold your job open, Ted," I said.

— — — — —

chapter

thirteen

The blazing tropical sun etched the scene around us in stark reliefs; the glaring planes and black valleys of the long swells, the piled, cottony billows of cumulous clouds that were scattered without pattern through the yellow-tinged sky. We cruised slowly, Strobel and the kid both on bow watch, alert for the grasping reefs and coral heads among which we sailed, knife-edged polyp structures of hard calcium that could gut a vessel from bow to stern and had cost many unwary mariners their lives. Ahead and behind, port and starboard, the pastel shapes rose towards the surface, seeming to sway and dance under the shimmering surface of the sea.

The ocean was alive; reefs are natural spawning grounds, and our progress disturbed shoal after shoal of colorful fish—many with the flashing brilliance and weird shapes of those found in fancier's aquaria. Now and again a flying fish leapt from the water, glided along above the surface on whirring pectorals, skipped to higher altitude by snapping its tail on the crest of a passing wave, then disappeared again into the sea. In the tropics I'd often found them high and dry on deck in the morning—even such high-decked vessels as destroyers.

Strobel shouted, the Pollack, spinning the wheel, threw the LOAFALONG hard to port, straightened only to dodge again as more coral swept past our sheer. Only slightly to the right a long white ledge of surf seemed to mark the end of the ocean—the mythical edge of the world, over which we'd topple if we approached too closedly. And there was something to the myth, perhaps—our world, at least, would end should we tear into the bottom-rending reef the breakers marked.

The sea was clear of traffic; the Owens hadn't gotten here—they could, I realized, be searching the wrong reef area altogether and might never catch up. Or possibly—but I doubted—they could be optimistic greenhorns touring the deadly reefs without realization of the hazards they faced.

"Boy!" Don exclaimed, "I've never been in the tropics before—this is rugged. And can you trust that new kid you've put on bow watch—that Harry Strobel?"

"He has to learn, and he's got the best of teachers. Relax," I laughed. "Don't *you* turn old-maidish on me, Don."

"I couldn't blame him," Buckley interjected. "I've faced a lot of knives and guns, but I've never been quite as tense as I am now. This could make an old man of me."

"It'll never make an old man of me," Gia surmised. "But I'm scared plenty. Wish I'd stayed sea-sick I wouldn't know what was going on."

"All of you," I said, noting that the whole crew wore swimsuits or sport trunks, "had better concern yourselves more with sun-burn than being disemboweled on coral. A few minutes in those outfits — unacclimated as you are — and you'll be doctor-bait. Incidentally, when we anchor down, I'll want some of you — especially you, Gia — on deck in swim gear. We might as well look like fishermen and swimmers loafing along the reef to any casual observers. While we're on the topic, I'll also want everyone not masquerading, below decks if visitors should show. I still haven't forgotten that Owens — "

"Who's getting old-maidish now, Jeff," Don laughed. "You spot some joker out looking for sailfish and worry about him on into the next day."

"I wouldn't have, if he'd taken the trouble to do what I just outlined. But no fishing-chairs, no fishermen, no lounging-gals-in-shorts — those guys were out on business."

"You're likely right," Buckley said, frowning. "But they have to find us — and know what we're here for."

"They'll know that — they've been doing everything to hold me in port-murder attempts, picket lines, phony arrest warrants; hell, they aren't under any illusions now and we may as well expect the worst."

An explosive clang, ear shattering in volume, shattered the converstaion; together we spun towards the wheelhouse to face Cookie, grinning over a galvanized wash tub and wooden salad-spoon. "Come and get it," he shouted, "before it gets cold."

Self-consciously, because of the start he'd given me, I led the way to the dining room and a breakfast of superlative ham, steak, eggs, and fried-potatoes, to forget, as I feasted, the torturous course we followed as I mulled a second cup of coffee. Rising, I replied, "Wheel."

A voice acknowledged thinly through the long brass pipe. "Think we see the hole you want — can you come up, Skipper?"

"Right with you, Pollack." I grabbed the cup and headed for the flying bridge. Red nodded a greeting, pointed ahead. I picked up binoculars and stared at the breach in the surf, at the more badly torn pattern beyond it.

"We're on third and going home, Red," I told him. "Take her through the reef, and cruise the edge of that white water beyond. I'll relieve Strobel for chow and Don and the rest can take the wheel and bridge for you. But after we're through; I don't want any mistakes."

"I can handle her until we anchor, Skipper. Unless you want to take it yourself. Don's a good seaman — but a better poker dealer and there's no one else I'd trust as far."

"Okay, Red. But I do want the bow until we see the VOLSTOK." I turned and climbed back to deck, wandered to the bow. Strobel was tense and white as he strained his eyes into the depths of the sea ahead, while my kid tender perched indolently on a bit, shoulders drooping, seemingly careless. He lifted his phone casually as I watched.

"Ten port," he announced wearily. Then "Straighten up, Pollack. Hard right, now. Okay, take her back." Through the maneuvers we'd dodged a series of rangy coral stems as little as a foot below the shimmering surface. My tender was worth his pay — outrageous as it was!

"Kid, Harry," I interrupted. "Go on down for breakfast. I'll cover for both of you."

"You'll need two just to replace me, Old Master!" the kid cracked, as Harry looked on, aghast at the liberties he took. "But if you want to sink the old scow, okay. I'm hungry as a bear. Come on, Harry, let's get our final meal while ole' weakeyes piles the tub up." He grabbed Strobel's arm, led him aft towards the gal-

ley as I picked up the headset and set muself to guid-
ing the boat through the thicket below us. A pair of
slim brown shapes flashed past; six foot barracuda
looking for their breakfast. This, I grinned wryly,
could make for some good diving.

Gia walked up and sat down beside me. She had
taken my advice, and changed the swim suit for a
white skirt and white long sleeved sweater. Dropping
her head on my shoulder, she asked gaily, "Or are you
afraid we'll damage the morale of your crew?" Above
the clean sea breeze wafted a tinge of perfume.

"Might improve it," I laughed. "Make them work
harder so they can change places with me someday.
You're a doll, Gia. Have I told you that you're a beautiful woman?"

"Hell no. You've been too busy playing cops and
robbers — or whatever it is. This is an improvement,
Skipper." Her eyes were sparkling, she tossed her head
to throw the gleaming mane across my face. The phone
buzzer sounded. I growled a reply.

"It's your scow and your girl, Skipper. But my neck
gives me a stake. Watch where you're going, Old
Master."

I said something profane, got a chuckle out of the
headset.

"I know all about it, Jeff," Gia laughed. "Someday
you're going to fire that wise kid. And that wise kid,"
she continued, "you saved on your last job by cutting
your own diving air line so you could get untangled
and get him to the surface before he suffocated."

"And did he tell you that he got himself into that
bind, saving my neck?" I asked.

"No. But Red told me. Jeff, you sure have a devoted
crew. They think you're about the only skipper — or
man — that ever lived. I sort of get the idea they'd do
anything for you — and vice-versa."

"Except to join the union," I grinned. "I don't think I could subrogate their morals to that extent."

A huge coral head loomed; I'd spotted it too late to dodge, ordered the Pollack to back down to turn around it. We minced by, the outcroppings missing our sides by bare inches as a crosswind blew us down on the reef. Then we were briefly clear, dodging an occasional small head, gaining foot by foot on the blue hole in the sheer wall off to the right. Finally it was alongside; the Pollack swung the bow hard right and we eased gently through to the lee-side of the long main reef line.

"It's a wonderful life," Gia sighed, oblivious to the hazards around us. "I wish — " she broke off the sentence, straightened up. I dropped an arm around her shoulder, drew her back to me.

"You wish?"

"That I'd met you sooner. Years sooner, Jeff. When — when maybe we could have made something of it. As is, I . . . I picked you up to quiz you for Clyde, and you let me — to quiz me about Chet and the Brotherhood and when it's all over, we'll both say goodbye with bad tastes in our mouths."

"Maybe. Maybe not. Are you playing a square game now, Gia?"

"Do you have to ask, Jeff?"

"Not really. But as long as you are, there's no-before where I'm concerned. Let's forget there was anything or anyone before we met — in fact. I've never even considered it. This is a lousy time for romancing though. If I let you distract me too much the kid'll have a point. Look — " I exclaimed, pointing off the port bow, Under the blue surface — not very deep -- lay a boat with a squared deck house and countered transom. Her high sheer was topped by a rangy foredeck; the hull was black.

"Stop all — no — back down a bit, Pollack," I called.

"We're here."

As air-clutches hissed and the big boat bucked under the lash of reversing propellors, the kid appeared on deck carrying a diving-lung, fins, faceplate, and weight-belt. He dropped them on the fantail and began unlashing a boarding-ladder as Red surveyed the bottom for holding ground and released the parrot-clip allowing the bow anchor to splash overboard. I appreciated this crew—more with every cruise; with every bonus and raise I added to their checks—whatever they got they deserved. The Pollack backed down, stretching anchor line ahead; Red and the kid dropped the stern anchor as well, led the boat forward to center between the pair of hooks as an extra holding precaution well advised this close to the reefs.

Finally the engines died, the pumps stopped their incessant whine; except for the chugging generator that supplied electricity for lights and refrigerators, the LOAFALONG was dead in the water, rocking and pictching lightly in the shelter of the coral wall just windward. I had strapped on the lung webs while the anchoring maneuvers were underway; now I strapped the weight-belt with its twenty-two pounds of lead rectangles into place, slid the face-mask on, and struggled with my swim-fins.

The kid appeared again on deck carrying another outfit—the two-bottled job for prolonged diving. "Just in case I have to bail you out, Old Master. Or would you rather I went along—you won't be needing a tender, and a safety man wouldn't hurt."

"Doubt I'll need a safety—this should be a straightforward job, but I'll be glad to have you stand by. And— if you're disappointed, don't—we'll have the work done before lunch; you'll have the rest of the day for sightseeing or whatever."

He returned my grin as I trod clumsily down the ladder, knees spraddled, fins flopping ludicrously. Diving gear adds to grace and maneuverability underwater, but it's a nuisance until you get it there. The balmy sea closed over my legs, I made the next couple of steps, released my hold, and sank slowly, erect, through the shadowless, transparent brine, breathing easily and tugging fins, belt, and lung-tank into comfortable positions as I went. A school of curious red snappers hovered around me; small ones from probably last spring's spawning. The gaily striped fish cavorted playfully through my airstream, letting the bubbles carry them towards the surface, then diving to return for another ride. They ignored gestures to frighten them, moving only inches out of range when I reached towards one. Suddenly, with a community mind, they wheeled and flashed away.

Glancing around I saw no cause for alarm, no barracuda or cruising shark to have triggered an alarm, and wondered, as always, about the social behavior and stimuli acting on these least known of all the world's creatures. It has been discovered only recently that fish make stylized sounds, that dolphins may well have a fairly sophisticated language; less is known even yet about the bottoms of our own seas than about the surface of the moon or the planet Mars.

My feet dropped onto the tan sand of the bottom, clean and firm as far as I could see. Walking towards the VOLSTOK, I gritted my teeth. She had been gutted; her bottom ripped from stem-to-stern on the ragged reef, Beyond that, she seemed intact, with sides, decks, and superstructure undamaged. And the skipper had talked of a squall! I circled the boat; she had not been too well cared for, I realized from the barnacle incrustations on her bottom. A couple of years overdue for drydock and bottom work, at least. Well — barnacles don't sink vessels. Coral polyps were already hard at work on the boat, attaching their little shelled communities that would grow one on another as the years passed, until the VOLSTOK became simply an undistinguishable part of the reef around it, without shape or identity beyond the surrealistic towers and battlements of hard calcium that enshrouded it.

That is another thing would be treasure hunters overlook — a vessel long sunk — an artifact of other times lying on the ocean floor — has no identity, no recognizable shape, nothing likely to attract attention of the searching seaman. The galleon, the treasure chest, the bow cannon, becomes merely another coral head sprouting out of the sea bottom, another rock of razor-edged fingers, providing convenient lurking spots for octopi, for vicious Moray eels. One more obstruction to sidestep as he continues his vain hunt for treasures that perception and dynamite might lead him to. Might — but probably not; the blasted object of his hunch could as well be just coral!

Completing a circle around the hulk, I sprang lightly to the foredeck, walked along the crusty surface to the wheelhouse. The hatch was closed; I tugged and fumed, finally moved it on rusty and corroded rollers. Entering, I found the bridge shipshape, made my way down a companionway into the hull. It was split with a lightless corridor leading fore and aft, with hatches opening into staterooms. The first hatch was free; it swung roughly to reveal a small compartment with double bunks, dresser,and its own head.

Light from two portholes illumined the space, and female garments strewn in disarray indicated tenancy. I lifted a skirt and stretched it without gain — it could have belonged to either of the Harrison women; mother or daughter; both were similar in size, and Emily had been as stylish a dresser as her daughter. Looking further, I slid open the top dresser drawer, extracted an ornate jewel box of ivory — inlaid ebony, and pried it open. Gems gushed from the box: broaches, pendants, rings, and necklaces. From memory I checked off a couple of pieces against the insurance list; this was one of my objectives! I crammed the jewelry back into the case, wedged it into the belt on my swim trunks, and left the compartment to the sea.

Another compartment had been Jan's stateroom, another the boys had shared. This latter contained a childish collection of sea shells scavenged from the remote Carribean beaches. One was a massive conch — the biggest I could remember. Neither this or Jan's room had anything of salvage worth; I re-entered the inky passageway and tried another door.

This stateroom was larger than the others with a scattering of male clothing, a corner gun case containing some uselessly rusted rifles and shotguns, and a desk to which a typewriter was clamped. There was a dicta-scriber bolted behind the machine and a small strong box, door ajar, secured between the desk and corridor bulkhead. I swung it open, again cussing salt water as the hinges fought rustily against my muscle.

There was a conglomeration in the little safe; reels of wire for the dictating machine, navigation aids, a couple of soggy — and empty cigar boxes, and a flexible plastic portfolio — a water and moistureproof case — similar to the one that contained the log book on my boat. An emulsion of dissolved paper fiber floated from the safe as I stirred the water within; under the slimy mess was a second plastic case, filled like the first. A study of the remainder of the stateroom revealed nothing of interest; hopefully I gathered the waterproofed packages and felt my way again through the black central corridor to the wheelhouse, where I deposited my loot.

The engine room was revealing; both engines were

throttled to full speed, with clutches engaged, when the vessel had torn across the reef and plummeted to the bottom where she lay now. Deliberate—of course; no sailor would run flat out, and at night, in shoaling water such as this. Probably the skipper had launched his dingy a quarter mile or so beyond the reef, opened the engines, and jumped before the doomed ship could accelerate dangerously. Probably, I decided, a hungry diver could make pay on salvaging the engines and shafts—the mills could be rebuilt, and the bronze re-used or sold at a high scrap price. But I wasn't that hungry.

I stopped at the wheelhouse to retrieve my trio of parcels, swam easily to the surface with slow leg strokes alone, and passed the packages to a waiting tender before I climbed aboard for the almost ritualistic Old Taylor and coffee—hardly needed in this moderate weather, but tasty nonetheless. I glanced at the wheelhouse clock; the whole search had taken barely fifteen minutes!

*   *   *   *

"One watch brooch," Ted Buckley read from the insurance list, in the privacy of my stateroom, "platinum case and mount. Circular mount with one and one-half carat blue-white fine diamonds, twelve total, set in clock positions."

"Check," I said.

"One necklace, platinum link with platinum-mounted three-carat diamond, blue-white, surrounded by thirty-carat cluster diamond cut blue-whites of approximate eighth-carat sizes."

"Check. I'd like to swipe this one."

"Yeah. This doll had a taste for ice. Pendant. Pear-cut emerald mounted on 24k gold. Square cut ruby above, surrounded by diamond cluster of eight-quarter carat stones."

"Check."

"That's about it, Jeff. The rest of the stuff isn't on this list. Do you have her insurance list?"

"I didn't bring it along, but I have it. Not as big a list — in value, at least, as these she had on approval. Bound to be here, I'd suppose; everything on the approval list is."

"What about the portfolios — we can do the honors of sealing and initialling the gems anytime — I don't expect you'll pilfer them anyhow — not with a police-witness especially." He grinned, slapped my leg.

"Thanks for the afterthought, Ted. I'll say something nice about you, someday too. Yeah — let's get into the bags — that's what I really came out after."

"Remember me? Me too."

"Cross your fingers, Ted." I tugged the zipper, broke the inner snaps loose. The inner zipper was clean and water-free; it slid easily on bright tracks. I spilled the pile of papers within on my desk, picked up the top sheaf of three pages, scanned it, and whistled. "Get a load of this, Ted." I offered the papers, picking up another batch. It was a magnificent job; names, dates, places, everything. Photostats of checks, a stolen copy of the union's strike-fund ledger showing vast withdrawals for the Florida real-estate ventures, others for loan-sharking use to tie members irrevocably to union command. There were affadavits — a couple of them dying statements — tying the union brass to lootings, murders, bombings, loan sharking, extortion, accepting money from shippers to assure them freedom from strikes. Five pages detailed — with evidence — Maurey's acceptance of twenty-thousand dollars payoff from one shipper to strike a competitor to shut him down. Later, again evidence, the payoff resulted in the bankrupt shipper's facilities being auctioned to the first by the receiver. For a pittance!

"We've got 'em!" I growled to Buckley, as we both leafed through the sheaf with the enthusiasm of kids with new toys. "We've got 'em."

"Yeah," Buckley laughed. "Bloody Maurey Nacchi, Logan, the works. Odd, though — there's nothing here on a couple; no mention of the Grissolms, nor of Nicky Lorraine. Of course, Harrison wouldn't have known anything about Grissolm — not and hired him as skipper. And he was a small fry crook in the outer ring, anyway. But Lorraine? We've got a bunch of them, though — that shyster that double-crossed the Senate Rackets Committee — this gets his tail in the well-known crack. And some Louisiana and Florida politicians. And cops," he sighed. "Always some goddam stinkin' cops that think the force is something to get rich in. Goddam double-crossing thieving cops! And I've gotta' haul them in — some of the guys I've worked fifteen, twenty years with. And a couple I didn't know about at that."

"You've nothing to be ashamed of, Ted. Your name wasn't on the list."

"But what does it do, Jeff? Not just to the police, but to the people they are supposed to protect. Who has any respect for a cop these days? Not a damned soul — and who can blame them when the papers keep carrying stories like this? One thieving-cop can ruin every man on every force in the country — cost them their respect as citizens, their respect as enforcers, their prestige of uniform. A story like this gets out, and every last one of us is a couple of steps lower on everyone's ladder. And here we can't even talk about one apple in a barrel — hell, we've got rot in two states and a dozen cities along the coast! So kids laugh at cops —

'Crime doesn't pay?' — they chortle — 'Just look at the long green that rookie in New Orleans knocked down. And he was just caught by accident — if that diver hadn't found the VOLSTOK he wouldn't have even gotten kicked off the force'. A crooked cop is a lot worse — immeasureably worse than a crooked crook — hell, he's a lousy hypocrite ignoring his oath, doubling against his duty, doing what he's being paid to keep people from doing. Like a preacher that gets caught in a vice-raid in a cat-house — what he does counts so heavy with people — so much more than if he were Joe Blow!"

"You're right, Ted. It wouldn't matter much to anybody if I got caught with the dice in my paw — but if it were you — neither you nor the force would ever live it down. There's one consolation, though, a cop will be turning in the cops. People will know there's at least one good man among them."

"Poor consolation. Hell. Some of these guys might as well be brothers — I grew up with them ... and old with them. Well —," he shrugged, "there's no choice. But I don't look forward to getting back from this cruise. Let's see what bad news we find in the other case."

I pulled it open, shook out more papers. And a diary. This was it — a solid stack of testimony and evidence against Nicholas 'Nicky' Lorraine. Mostly rough stuff. He'd been the one who'd organized — and frequently played a personal hand in — the murders, bombings, vandalisms, and terrorism. The stacking story told not only of a man doing a criminal job — but of one doing it for the sheer love of it.

Sadistic, merciless, a torturer whose tortures continued after need for them faded by the victim's compliance. A killer who killed when his purposes could be better served by sparing his victims. Lorraine's tortures were often unique; he adapted ancient Oriental,

Egyptian, and European methods to his service with relish. An affidavit of an ex-Brotherhood member in hiding in Cuba detailed the death of a non-conformist by the Seven Heavenly Gates of oriental fame. The man, naked and handcuffed, had been placed in a coffin-sized cage of heavy wire mesh, divided into eighths by wire screens. Into the end at his feet were turned a dozen ravenous wharf rats, carefully starved for several days. Then a little later, the first screen was lifted. And another. From time to time new rats were added.

Two days later, wrapped in canvas and chains, the remains were dropped into the Mississippi from a garbage barge. Three of the Brotherhood men, and a State Prisons Parole and Corrections Officer were compelled to observe — also handcuffed — by way of warning. Lorraine, the affadavit concluded, had shown a garish excitement through the show — a writhing, moaning, shaking, sensual display that had sickened the observers nearly as much as the feature performance he'd produced! I shuddered as I passed the flimsies to Buckley, who scanned it in silence, and dropped it, face ashen.

Carefully I slid the first batch into their repository, then the second. Pausing, I flipped open the diary, glanced through pages devoted to the beauties of the islands, the size of fish caught, the usual amusing faux-pas occurring on rolling boats with food, drinks and the like. Then the mood changed; I read the lines of heart-break that followed with effort, silently offered the manuscript to Buckley. He studied it with increasing incredulity, finally flipped it shut and handed it back.

"And I thought I had troubles," he muttered. Nodding my assent, I slid the volume into its smooth plastic wrap, tossed the pair of packages onto my desk.

"Let's get some fresh air. And maybe whiskey to clean the taste in our mouths," I said.

———————

chapter

fourteen

Gia's bikini might have been a bit less colorful than my outfit that my wiseacre tender had described as a loincloth, but I wouldn't lose her in the water, I thought as I piloted the outboard speed hull I used as a service-boat for the LOAFALONG towards a minute hole in the reef-marking surf. I throttled back, saw the water was deep enough for the little boat, and jammed the throttle open. The hull leapt up and forward, dropping to a planing attitude, skimming the crest of the sea as it slapped and spanked on the shallow waves.

Gia tensed, then relaxed as the boat hurtled along, its speedometer hovering between thirty and thirty-five knots. I held it at the pace for the sheer love of speed, the exhilaration of feeling wind and spray slam into my face, stinging and biting. Finally I swung reefward again in a long circle and snapped the throttle to idle.

The boat braked with an abruptness than threw us

forward in the Naugahide seat; our wake overtook us, sloshing over the transom into the boat. Mincingly now, I edged again into the reef, let the engine die with an indignant spit, and tossed a light Danforth anchor over the side.

"Whew!" Gia exclaimed. "I thought we were going swimming before we planned. This thing can go."

"You've never water-skied?" I asked.

"I tried once behind a fishing boat – sort of. Couldn't ever get up on the skis, though."

"Not enough speed. Get on them behind this boat and you can't help but come up – she'll pull a pair of skiers almost out of the water as fast as you hit the throttle. We'll try a little skiing tomorrow if the weather holds – I'll have you acting like a pro in the first half hour."

"Sounds great to me. But I'm more anxious to see what fish look like from close up. How do you get into these rigs, anyhow?"

I helped her with the bottles; latching the web buckles across her halter took a while – and not because they were corroded. She turned and grinned back at me.

"Troubles, Jeff?" she chided.

"Lots of troubles, Gia. If I fumble once more it'll be too dark to dive before I get through."

"You were fumbling?" She dropped her head on my shoulder, caught my hands and cupped them tightly over the barely covered breasts. "If you were fumbling," she muttered, "I'm ready for a serious try. But I don't know if – not underwater!"

"Who knows?" I shrugged, "unless they try."

"You'd try anything once, wouldn't you, Jeff?" Her voice was musing. I tipped her lips up to mine.

"Probably once too often," I acknowledged shakily, a long minute later. "If we're going to dive, we better get at it. If not, we could move up the reef beyond binocular range..."

"Don't be so impatient," Gia laughed, tossing her head. She slipped on a mask and fins as I clambered into my gear. I gestured toward the transom, balanced the boat as she swung over and dropped in, still holding the transom edge.

"Come around to the side and balance while I get off," I warned as I swung over the opposite gunwale, barely rocking the little glass hull as I slid into the warm sea. I dodged under the boat, caught her leg and pinched, watching her jerk and struggle with glee, until she realized I wasn't a barracuda.

"That was mean," she teased as I surfaced beside her.

"Just indoctrination—never get excited in the water."

"With you around—how do I manage," she laughed.

"Don't be impudent. Or impatient. Or is that your line?"

I explained briefly the operation of the lung, watched her take her first few nervous breaths with it. Finally she nodded her readiness, I motioned downward, and tipped into a long surface dive, glancing back to see her stroking easily after me.

Her face contorted; I saw her swallow to clear her ears—always a problem for tyros who tend to panic as ear pressure fails to follow water and builds painfully at even moderate depths. I wheeled to a standing position, caught her hand as she made the twenty-foot bottom and stood motionless, breathing hard as she let her nerves settle. At the rate those lungs were pulsing, I realized, she'd run out of air fifteen minutes ahead of me. With a grin of encouragement, I slid my arm around her waist, led her gently forward as she tried to learn to walk on the bottom, instead of leaping in the new buoyant world she was discovering.

The surface looked like crinkled cellophane from below; the blazing sun above left the reef towering beside us an etching in rose, buff and white. It massed, it branched, it writhed, it curved and recurved according to the whims of its almost microscopic builders. Here and there deep slots and holes showed as black blotches, again we passed a spot the little creatures had bridged, for some reason disdaining the sand at that point for foundation use.

I restrained Gia abruptly, and pointed. From a black patch emerged what looked at a glance like only another coral branch—but one that suddenly moved, then stopped. A little brown skate, cousin to mighty Manta rays, loitered along the bottom, winged-sides flapping rhythmically as he searched for small shellfish—also the principal food of Mantas. He approached the tentacle, ignoring the seemingly lifeless mollusk as part of the background. There was a flurry; the tentacle lashed past the hapless skate, catching it with powerful vacuum cups as it struggled ineffectually. A second snaked out of the hole, a third. Then the ugly center body and head, bumpy and warty, with its deep-set, mournful eyes that look myopic but are possibly more of the vicious creature's useful illusions.

The octopus remained moored by spare tentacles to the coral lair as his tooth-filled mouth obscured the little skate. There was a thin streamer of blood in the water, and the monster darted back into his hole— the exploratory tip of tentacle emerging moments later. Gia looked pale—such spectacles usually leave viewers weak initially, but the sea is the sea—it holds all of its creatures—if loosely—within its confines; here they must live, feeding on whatever presents itself, in an eat or be eaten existence in which neither small nor large can escape some hungry contender. I doubted the mollusk would attack us; he was too small to be so ambitious, but shied away anyhow as we passed his lair in the reef base. The tentacle fluttered expectantly as we passed, then reverted to somnolence.

Like migrating Monarch Butterflies, a swarm of small Angel fish descended on us, fluttering about us curiously, nosing at us, then darting back. Gia was entranced by the brilliant triangles with their black and yellow stripes, I laughed as she tried to catch one of the seemingly fearless fish and came away with a fistful of brine. The fish followed us as we walked a few steps, but darted away in terror as a four-foot Grouper, scarlet and white, nosed his way toward us at shoulder height. I wished for a phone; all I could do on this tour was point and hope to identify and explain the species later.

A long shape darted by above us; thin and menacing. A barracuda, but small, I guessed—perhaps four feet long. Even close at hand it's hard to define the 'cuda; their speed, slim streamlining, and nearly solid color renders them little but a dark streak in the sea. Perhaps he'd come back; the fish have curiosities as insatiable as their appetites; often I've had them face me from five or six feet, only to dart away if I moved a hand abruptly. But not for long—in moments curiosity would again override their fear, and they'd dart back to continue their vigil with increased courage.

Sea life is graduated—as it is on land. In open seas, whales and dolphins, the bigger sharks, squid, and octopi range over thousand mile voyages in search of prey and mates, while smaller fish live in the shallows, among the reefs and kelp, and in the bottom mud of coastal shoals. Anywhere in the sea some life can be observed, if only the microscopic plankton—possibly almost as much vegetable as animal—that clutter the surface and flouresce when disturbed at night.

Along the reefs, though, the sight-seeing is at its spectacular best. Here the polyps build their fans and castles, and the squatters find shelter from stormy seas, from depredations of bigger fish, and from the hazards they pose for each other. At the reef's base, the weird shell-bound life flourishes; sponges, oysters and clams, conchs and perriwinkles, the hermit crabs that borrow shells from dead builders, an occasional octopus — horror of the mollusk family, sea urchins whose long spines break off in an unwary diver's foot to cause throbbing, painful infections.

Above and around are the fish, in profusion and in color; fish drab and green, or brown, or black; fish splattered with blotches of crimson and blue, fish thick and thin, smooth and warty, graceful and clumsy. Fish that swim, fish that fly, and fish that flap their way through the water like a gull gliding in a head-wind.

Through the teeming jungle we interlopers browsed, big feet stirring the bottom sand in little whirls, exhaust air crashing about out ears, and burbling to the surface in twin streams through which fish from time to time played.

I checked my watch; time was running out for in this airless world, people too are imprisoned and restricted; limited in scope to the amount of air they bring with them on their backs. Grudgingly I led Gia back toward the boat, we swam lazily to the surface, returning to a workaday world from the fantastic one outside and beyond it.

"I never knew, Jeff," Gia gasped as I tugged her into the outboard, helped her gladly with the recalcitrant lung straps, "that things like—fish—were so beautiful."

"They aren't on the market counters. Most of them lose their color and change somewhat in shape in the first few minutes they're out of the water. To see them as they really are, you have to visit them at home."

"Jeff," Gia exclaimed, "can we go down again? Please?"

"Tell you," I mused. "If Ted and the crew have no objection, we'll cruise on over to Andros Island. It's nearest – at least the nearest inhabited spot – to the great reef that stretches past it into the Carribean. Only one in the world bigger is the Great Barrier Reef off Australia – that one is something like three thousand miles long, but the Andros Reef is impressive enough, to say the least. We'll get a cabin at Andros Town and explore the reef for a week or two if you'd like. I don't think there's too much rush about getting back with our story. Hell, the people have been at this racket for years, another week or two won't matter a lot and they'll probably be mostly lying low. They won't risk much violence until the smoke clears and they know where they stand."

"Could we, Jeff? Oh, could we?" She was in my arms; it was minutes before I had the freedom to breathe or accede. Finally I hit the start button, swept the speedboat in a long circle through the reef and back to the LOAFALONG.

The crew had been enjoying the lazy day and lazy weather, too. Buckley was splashing and slogging across a coral head close by, spear gun in hand, face-plate obscuring his hawk-nose, with Don Miller keeping pace. Red Price flashed through the air in an ill-concieved swan dive from the bow and splatted heavily into the water, a high spout of froth marking his point of entry.

The kid had vanished; as I reached the deck, a burble of air bubbles along the reef's fringe showed his occupation, while Harry and Cookie loafed on a drifting raft with fishing poles. The Pollack swam mightily toward the raft—"Thank God the anchors are holding," I muttered under my breath as I realized no one was keeping store. Not that it mattered, really; any of the crowd could swim or paddle back fast enough to catch the boat should it begin dragging the two big hooks.

Gia was exhausted—more emotionally from the newness of skin diving, I surmised, than from the exertion. Dropping onto the deck she stretched luxuriously, grinned up at me, and closed her eyes. I took a long fast dive off the fantail, broke water half-way to the coral head, and stroked over to join Ted and Don. It didn't take long—about as long as to offer the suggestion of vacationing on Andros—for the pair to agree with enthusiasm.

"I think you're proselyting, Jeff," Buckley told me, sternly. "With or without malice aforethought, you're making a waterfront bum or sailor of me. Hell's Bells. How do you expect me to go back to work after this?"

"I don't expect me to—so why should you be any different?" I laughed. "Anyhow, Ted. I'll keep holding your job open."

I swam back to the LOAFALONG, flopped on deck beside Gia. Through the rest of the afternoon the pattern remained, swimming and loafing under the benign tropical sky.

—————

chapter

fifteen

The morning sky was obliterated by thick fog. We checked engines and equipment in the early hours, waiting for it to burn off and commiserating for the pilots of planes occasionally passing invisibly overhead as we lay safely at anchor, unneedful of coping with the hazards of fog-bound navigation or landings. One of the bilge pumps was leaking; I replaced the packing, changed some starter-box contacts, generally caught up on odds and ends that normally await port, but could as well be done aboard the dead ship now.

Don worked with me on machinery, while the rest of the crew touched up paint on deck, tied line splices, and generally tidied up. The fog thinned by nine o'clock, half an hour later it had thinned to wisps; by ten the sun blazed again through the clear tropical sky. I debated between staying through the day, and cruising on to Andros, decided finally to go on, and started up the big diesels. The whole crowd accumulated in the wheel house as the throbbing plants warmed, enthused and eager.

"We'll be able to cut straight over to Andros Island, and run along the coast to Andros Town," I said. "Ought to be able to make it by dark. I'd as soon not cruise these shallows at night unnecessarily." Above the muted throbbing of the idling diesels, I heard a growing roar. Glancing out a wheelhouse window I saw the airplane—a Stearman biplane of WWII vintage—slanting down out of the sun, its wings and struts silhouetted blackly against the burning orb.

"Just like the Corsairs in Chesapeake Bay," I noted, as it hurtled toward us. "When I first was cruising up there, they scared me silly, buzzing my ship. Finally I got used to it, then one caromed off another tub in our formation, and I wound up scared all over again." The ship rushed at a bare sixty or seventy feet above us; as it passed, a black shape dropped from it, splashed to the water a few yards behind, and beyond us.

Instants later, a tall column of smoke and water towered upward from the center of the ripple, the LOAFALONG was staggered as though struck by a massive fist! Then the boom of the explosion shook the boat, rattling the wheelhouse windows. Gia and Harry were hurled to the floor by the blast; my head slammed painfully into a coaming. Some of the others came away only a little better.

"My aching—" Red's ejaculation merged into a profane stream.

"He'll come around again!" the kid shouted.

Looking up, I realized he was right. The Stearman was climbing in a long, gentle turn—best for combined altitude gain and course reversal. The Pollack had grabbed a carbine from the gun rack; he slammed open the breech to check the load, and handed it to me, reaching for another for himself. Everyone followed his lead snatching every available gun, rifle or shot.

"Don't waste ammo," I admonished. "Only way you

can hit him is when he's coming in and close. Red. Pull the stern anchor fast—I'll be able to maneuver a little against the bow." Red Price rushed to the fantail as I clutched the engines astern to give his cable slack enough. The kid joined him, dropping his rifle on the deck, and struggling mightily to get the hook aboard as the Stearman's turn tightened for its next approach. He wouldn't be as likely to miss the second time I reflected with a grimace.

Red waved. I saw the big Danforth come over the stern, lines askew. They dropped the hook and retrieved their arms, dashing for the wheel house as I shoved windows open. Only Strobel lacked a weapon.

"Harry," I said, taking a hopeless gamble, "When I shout, push both of these buttons marked 'neutral,' release them, push the ones marked 'forward,' then jam both throttles forward. When I shout again, close throttles 'neutral, astern,' and full throttle again. Got it?"

"Aye, Sir," the boy answered proudly and properly over the crescendoing roar of the Stearman's big radial engine. She was clip-winged and over-powered another of the southern Florida crop of dusting ships. I pointed my rifle at the base of the number one cylinder, but held fire while the others followed my lead. Closer the ship came; I saw the pilot leaning far over the cockpit cowl, gauging his distance, wanting to get us this time.

"Now, Harry," I shouted, as my rifle cracked and the crew followed with a virtual broadside of small arms. I heard air hiss, clutches slam in the engine room, the throaty snarl of my big 'Jimmy' engines. The boat lunged forward. If only the props don't snag the anchor cable, I thought, as the rifle cracked and bucked against my shoulder. Still the Stearman closed, trying desperately to turn shallowly to follow the boat, but too low to make it. The second bomb dropped blackly from the cockpit as the propellor-arc, silver against the sky, vanished. The unloaded engine screamed shrilly as it wound up, the fuselage abruptly was enveloped in a brilliant ball of orange.

There was a second blast; the airplane disintegrated into a shower of black jagged parts that rained across our deck and overhead. Shrapnel shrilled through the open windows as we ducked; the LOAFALONG staggered, leapt again, rolled violently as shock waves of one, then another, and a third explosion rocked her. The pilot of the aircraft dropped stonelike into the sea near the reef, the engine hurtled on to splash a couple of hundred yards away.

"Back, Harry!" I yelled belatedly. Calmly the boy followed the order—smoothly going through the all-important 'neutral' buttons, without which the engines would not reverse. I was astonished as the big boat slid smoothly back.

"Stern anchor out if the bow lines not fouled," I added. Red and the tender dragged themselves from the wheelhouse deck, and headed astern. Moments later they signalled the anchor bottomed; I took the wheel and powered the boat into the center of its tethers.

"Stop all," I called. "We'll have to check for damage—and maybe try to look at that pilot if the sharks don't beat us to the punch." Don disappeared into the engine room, moments later the machinery was again silent.

"Red," I called. "You and the crew check the hull for damage. Harry. For the little time you've been aboard, you handled the LOAFALONG like an expert. You deserve a slap on the back."

"Thanks, Skipper." Harry grinned broadly and made a mock salute. He figured he belonged now.

"I'm going to find the pilot, if I can manage it. Gia—

why don't you and Cookie mix up an early lunch—
make mine several good strong highballs. I'll be back
before the ice melts." I dropped my yacht cap on the
panel cowl, slid on fins, walked to the rail, and took a
long dive over the side, emerging to swim slowly to
the area in which the pilot had sunk.

I swam with a long, easy crawl, keeping my face
under water and watching the bottom as I went. I'd
remembered right; a black shape lay on the shallow
bottom below me. Arching into a surface dive, I slid
through the water, stared closely at the explosion and
fire-blackened face without recognition. I searched
his pockets, extracted a billfold and swam back to the
surface, reaching it breathless and panting. Too many
cigarettes. Should be good for at least a minute and
a half at that depth; I doubted the whole dive had taken
sixty seconds. I swam leisurely back, found the kid
had thoughtfully rigged the boarding ladder in my
short absence.

In the wheelhouse, I opened the wallet, glanced at
the airman's certificate, driver's license, and sundry
credit and business cards. With a sardonic grin I
shuffled the stuff to Buckley, who stood at my elbow.

"We've really got them going, Ted," I laughed.
"They're sending their first string onto the field now."
The name on the papers was an impressive one to
me: "Reginald Miles Logan!"

"Yeah. Big gun for sure. Scratch one I could have
arrested. Damn you, Jeff. You never leave any for me."

"You'll have plenty left over this time, buddy boy.
Cops, politicos, and, I suppose, the rest of the Brotherhood gang—though there are one or two I'd beat you
out of if I could."

Red entered. "Kid and I have been all over the outside, Skipper. And Pollack and Don have checked her
inside. No indication of open seams; doesn't seem

to be taking water anyplace."

"Good. Too late to go into Andros now. We may as well spend another day coasting along here, and leave in the morning."

"Does that mean we'll have more bomber raids?" Gia pondered.

"Not much chance. Oh — I saw one of the bombs, down near the pilot — it was a home-made job, dozen sticks of dynamite taped together with a powder fuse. I imagine a tank and at least one bomb blew when we shot him down. But no — they'll not try that again — and certainly not today. It'll be tomorrow at least before they are even able to find out how this try came off." I lit a cigarette. "Relax, everyone. No watch, no work details." I picked up one of the highballs Gia had prepared without argument — good gal, this one — most of them fought over my choice of lunches.

"Can we dive along the reef, again, Jeff?"

"No reason why not. Let's try it out further up, though. The communities along it will vary from place to place — likely we'll find something different from yesterday's sights as Gary is from New York."

chapter

sixteen

The little Cornelius air compressor in the engine room had worked most of the night filling diving bottles with twenty-six hundred pounds of air apiece, but at that, I doubted that we'd have enough for the crowd. Today everyone had decided to try their hands on the ocean floor; Buckley, frog-footed and masked, stood at the LOAFALONG's rail as Gia and I swept away in the speedboat.

My kid tender had already taken Harry Strobel in hand; with lungs and spear-guns they had disappeared almost as quickly as I'd given the word to go. The rest of the crowd were variously dispersed, in and under water.

Picking a spot along the reef at random, far from the big boat and its crowded confusion, far from the wreckage of the Stearman and its dead pilot, I swung in and shut down the engine. Holding an anchor in the reef is never a problem; I simply swam down with the hook and lodged it in a hole in the coral, returned

to pick up my lung and settle Gia into hers. Finally
we dropped to the bottom for another safari into the
strange and different world so few people know.

The miniature architects here had gone hog-wild;
interspersed among the stemmy cliffs of coral were
fern-like structures of delicate hues, each fern leaf a
fan of exquisite lacework, veined and slotted with a
geometric perfection. The fan tops were scalloped
at the tops, with constantly changing radii to add to
the strength of the seemingly paper-thin structures.
Each of the fan blades was twelve or fifteen feet tall.
The structures dwarfed us as we wandered among
them.

The water was thick with small, brilliant fish; I
couldn't classify them, but they bore a resemblance to
the trigger fish of Hawaii, and were striped with
reds, yellows and blacks like the clown barbs long
favored by aquarists. The fish schooled so thickly we
had to wave them away from our faces to maintain
vision. Lobsters also abounded. The big crustaceans
were comical as they backed skittishly away from us
waving their massive pincers menacingly as they fled.
Pop-eyed females with foot-long antennae crowded
around the claw-equipped males for what questionable
protection they afforded.

I tipped into swimming posture, sneaking up behind
one nearly a foot and a half long. Seizing it behind its
claws, I returned to Gia, the lobster threshing and
clacking his pincers. His eyes rotated wildly in their
sockets as he sought some avenue of escape. The creatures are not to be underrated; the big jaws can
inflict painful and occasionally serious damage to
fingers and toes if given a chance to wrap the bony
serrated pincers around extremities. Finally I turned
him loose; he swam to the bottom and scuttled away,
running backwards. Gia laughed too hard; she lost

her mouthpiece, and retrieved it with a display of near panic.

Sensing a form above, I looked up and pointed. A Manta Ray, probably the most terrible spectacle under the sea, was approaching just above us. He was easily ten feet across, flat-bodied and blunt nosed, with a long trailing tail, barbed throughout its length. Rays swim by flapping the fins along their sides up and down in bird-like fashion; their size, massive build, somber color, and barbed tail make them a completely frightening sight. The monster's appearance is deceptive. Mantas are essentially harmless, sluggish, creatures, who support themselves by eating shellfish which they crush easily in their massive jaws, spitting small piles of shells in neat pyramids along the sea floor.

Gia seemed to shrink as she watched the monster, frozen in incredulity by the spectacle. He flapped his way on past, to disappear in the distance. She shook her head and shuddered; I caught her hand and guided her on up the reef, around the gaping shells of a massive scalloped clam. These *were* dangerous; if stepped into by an unwary diver, the foot and a half wide shell with its iron-tough muscle would snap shut in instants, trapping the victim's foot until he drowned or suffocated, to wind up in classical undersea tradition as feed for the scavenging fish. Pressure of water we stirred in our path must have startled the biped; the great upper shell closed abruptly, accumulated seaweed and bottom sand whorling around it as the motion shook it clean. A couple of dozen table-sized ocean trout fled past, possibly running from the ray, or from a preying barracuda; I wished for a spear gun but couldn't have managed a shot anyhow—startled fish are far too fast.

Gia's respiration had been about normal this trip;

her air had held up as long as mine, as she'd quickly acclimated herself to the feel of this world and dropped back to normal breathing. But mine was about done; the warning buzzer set to six minutes warning was grinding against my arm. Grudgingly I turned back; we rose toward the reef top and our speed boat as breathing got tight with diminishing air bottle pressure. The sun was still high; probably we could pick up a couple of spare bottles, if any were left, or perhaps recharge ours if necessary, in time for another dive later in the afternoon. I helped Gia out of her rig, and commented on the possibility for more diving time.

"It would be wonderful, Jeff, I'm sold—completely. I've never seen or even visualized anything like this. So beautiful—and yet sort of eerie, too."

"Probably the fish figure we add an eerie atmosphere," I laughed. "For them their world doubtless seems quite normal." I hit the speedboat starter; the whine of the accelerating engine killed all opportunity for conversation as the boat hurled sea away from its bow and roared homeward.

As we sped down the reef, with the LOAFALONG looming bigger, I realized we were in trouble. Tied alongside my boat was a familiar white and mahogany shape—the big Owens I'd been watching two days ago.

I shrugged mentally; in a fifteen-foot outboard, there was no other place to go!

----

chapter

seventeen

Gia looked queryingly at me as I throttled back slightly to give myself an extra moment to speculate. I replied with a shake of the head and leaned closer to her.

"I feel like little Johnny when his girl friend said yes; he said 'desus cwis — wha'da I do now?' " I told her. "We can't go anywhere else; we have to go aboard and play it by ear." I swung towards the LOAFALONG's port side, tied the speedboat to the boarding ladder and helped Gia aboard. To face Bloody Maurey Ippacchi. And his .45 Colt. And a handful of strangers. And their guns. And a beautiful girl whom I'd last seen sunburned and disarrayed. The girl I'd stolen from the Carribean. Jan Harrison.

"Meet my friends," Maurey sneered. "Clyde, Davey, Nicky, Bennie, Shultzy." He nodded at them in turn, but the forty-five stayed fixed.

"And Mrs. Nicholas Lorraine," I added. "You missed her, Maurey."

"How did you know?" Jan demanded, gasping. I glanced around as I prepared a reply. Buckley, unarmed and still in trunks, Red and Pollack, Cookie, Don Miller—they had all of us at gunpoint except Harry and the kid.

"Doesn't matter," Maurey snapped at her. "Not now." To me he said, "All right, Tyler. It's over. Gimme the stuff you found, and we'll be on our way."

"With a few more corpses to feed the fish. Sorry, Maurey."

"Who said anything about corpses?" Lorraine demanded. "No one said they were going to kill you."

"No one told Rick and Emily Harrison that they were going to be killed to keep their testimony out of court, either, Nicky," I said. "But that's the way you worked it out. And you were a damned fool to do it. Maurey thought he was safe as long as you were married to Jan and you had a perfect chance to cut his throat—the way you've tried to for years. Harrison had about decided—from what he said in his diary— to give you a break and dump the evidence against the rest while ignoring yours. You could have let him live and come out better. Or was it like the guy you fed to the rats—was it so much fun to kill him that you were willing to stand the losses?"

"But how did you know?" Jan demanded. "About us?"

"I just told you. It was in your father's diary— packed away with the evidence of Nicky's murders and tortures—"

"Shaddup," Lorraine demanded, menacing me with his gun.

"Go on," Jan insisted. "I want to hear this, Nicky."

"You will regardless, Jan. I knew long before that. You recovered from your sunburn and exposure too quickly to have been on the raft as long as you said. Maurey got a big bang out of the very idea that your father might cross him; he figured him for a tame bear after you married Lorraine. And there's one thing more — an erstwhile friend of mine tried to con me into this job without my knowing it. I think I know why."

"Get up here," Lorraine's voice grated as he looked over the LOAFALONG's rail. The kid pulled himself up the boarding ladder, leaning under the weight of his lung bottle. Harry followed, impeded still more by CO_2 spear gun he carried.

"If you'd invited me to the party," the Kid quipped to me, "I'd have brought my dinner jacket." He lined up obediently, though, looking grimmer than his gag indicated.

"Sure nice I got your whole mob, Tyler," Lorraine laughed, sneeringly. "I love to fix up wisecrackers and trouble-makers."

"I'll recommend you to my friends. At any rate, Jan, it was pretty obvious almost from the beginning. You didn't have anyone fooled. Not any more than Maurey or Nicky."

"Mr. Lorraine. I don't rate you as a friend."

"Which is an all time understatement, Nicky. As you'll find out when they throw the switch, if you last that long."

"You talk big for being in such a little position."

"Nicky!" Jan demanded, "is this all straight?"

"Hell. You think I'm a boy scout, or something. Get wise, kid."

"I think you're a gone goose," I answered for her. "Real gone. You ought to see that evidence. Affidavits, photostats of checks, the works. And the tortures that boy of yours loves to inflict...."

"Like the beat said in his obit.," the kid cracked, "don't dig me now, Daddy-o, I'm real gone this time."

"Where's the stuff?" Ippachio demanded. "Let's get this business settled."

"Reckon we ought to give it to them, Red?" I asked. He grimaced, spat on the deck for reply. "I don't think my crew wants me to turn it loose, Maurey," I answered. Lorraine stepped toward me, lashed out with his free hand. The blow caught me on the side of the face. Despite my quick roll a flash of blinding pain smashed my senses for an instant. The fist flicked again doubling me.

"Now?" he demanded. I spat—but not at the deck. His splattered face contorted with insane rage; he swung again. I felt myself falling but couldn't even break my fall as I crashed heavily to the deck. Gia screamed; I heard oaths from Buckley and Red. Slowly my head cleared. I dragged myself to my knees, managed to stand again. Six of them. And guns. Damn! We were dead—didn't have a chance. I could maybe find a break to get one or two of them if I led them down to get the evidence; it would split them and if only a couple came along... Or better, one. I studied the crowd; they were all pros. No tension, no excitement, no rattling by my taunts. Even splitting them there was little chance. But otherwise none at all.

"I think I can convince you real quick," Lorraine snapped. "You damned tough guys take a lot of punishment, but your girl—and I have a bone to pick with the Gia doll anyhow—seems like the cat changed her stripes somewhere along the way." He leered at Gia, stepped toward her, reaching with his free hand. I chopped swiftly at it, he howled and jerked back, spinning on me.

"Hold it," I told him quietly. "Even with guns you may not win a riot, Nicky. And I'm about to start it if you touch the girl."

"Do I get the papers, Tyler?"

"Maybe. I'll make a deal. If you—and your gun— have guts enough to come below with me alone—and you live through it, yes; you get the papers."

"No. He doesn't get the papers. Stand still. All of you!" The voice crackled with tension, brittle and harsh, practically a gasp. Jan's hand was steady, though, as she pointed the cocked forty-five at her compatriots. "I didn't know, I didn't know, I didn't know," she cried hysterically. "I believed you, Nicky— that it was the jewels. I believed you, God help me. Now—drop your guns."

Nicky Lorraine sneered at his wife, but made no effort to turn. "Don't be a fool. You couldn't get more than one or two of us if you had nerve enough to pull the trigger at all. Drop the heater, Jan, and face the facts. You're with us—and couldn't get out if you wanted to."

"Lie, Nicky," I snapped. "She's out. I've known that from the start, too. Or nearly."

"And you," another tense voice, sibilant with its strain and hate whispered. "You killed my father, Lorraine." Harry Strobel still held the spear gun, but leveled now at Lorraine's abdomen. "I am going to kill you now, Mr. Lorraine." There was a hiss as carbon dioxide blasted from the cylinder and into the firing chamber. There was a flash in the sun; Lorraine stood staring stupidly, incredulously, at the thick steel shaft that protruded from his belly, with barb dripping blood, emerging from his back. He clutched the shaft, and dripped on the buff deck. All of us stood for an instant, dumbfounded, then I leaped for his gun, wrenched it from nerveless fingers, and triggered two shots at Maurey who staggered backward under the massive impact of the big slugs, somersaulted across the lifelines, and splashed into the sea. He had made no sound.

The rest of the crew were in motion now, as I fired at random at our assaulters. Two or three shots obliterated the face of the one called Shultzy; I lost track as the red film of rage that clouded my vision, the moving figures, and blasting guns, tore at my reason. Lead shrilled, guns cracked, the forty-five bucked in my hand like something living.

Then there was silence. My vision cleared, my reason returned. The gun I held was empty; still I clutched it from force of habit. Red stood near the fantail, holding a smoking revolver. Pollack stood near him, holding a smoking automatic. Don Miller stood by the wheelhouse holding Jan Harrison Lorraine. Both of them were smoking judging by the intensity of their embrace. Harry lay prostrate on deck. The kid held a fish gaff, its sharp hook dripping blood. Buckley too was prone. Four hoodlums lay grotesquely, bleeding and dead. Lorraine still stood, still clutched the steel shaft from which blood still poured like water from a faucet. His eyes glazed as I watched. Slowly his legs buckled, and he collapsed on deck.

Buckley stirred, moaned. "Goddammit, Tyler," he snarled, "did you save one for me?" He dragged himself to his feet, rubbing a bleeding lump on his head, and surveyed the corpses on deck. "That's the story of my life," he sighed heavily and bleakly, "you were there first."

I bent over Harry, the hero of the moment. His breath was shallow, a pool of blood ran from beneath him. Turning him gently, I found the wounds—a shallow groove across his chest, a bullet hole completely through his upper right leg, clean and relatively harmless. He'd make it. Gently I lifted him, carried him below, and stretched him on a table. I had opiates in the medical cabinet; it took only minutes to shoot in a syrette of morphine, dust sulfa on the wounds, shoot a shot of penicillin into him, and bandage all the damages. He'd need a doctor, but that could wait 'til Andros; he'd be all right.

On deck, the crew were cleaning up. Rolling hoodlums overboard, hosing off blood, tossing cartridge shells into the sea, and cleaning bloody gaffs and spears. I stopped at the wheelhouse hatch to watch momentarily, turned to the radio-phone and called Laird's.

"Gaylord," a sales type voice responded from a thousand mile distance.

"Tyler. I've been told—been approached, I think you or your crooked private eyes would say—to negotiate with you on the VOLSTOK gems. Sorry I couldn't have salvaged them under contract; it would have been cheaper; I'm told the price for recovery is fifty grand, and I'll have to arrange my fee for my services. Dealing with crooks is dangerous; it'll be high. Interested?"

His profanity was competent.

"You're on radio, Gaylord," I finally managed to interject. "Remember your public—and that the phone company will cancel your service for language of that sort. I'll talk over the details when I get back, but thought you'd want to know."

"You can't fool me, Tyler. You've been to the VOLSTOK. What can you give me on its condition; should we pay claims? What about the private jewelry? Did you find it? What's the score?"

"We've no financial arrangements to reimburse me for making reports on my findings. I did salvage a crewless Owens while I was out here; she's alongside now, so I'll make a little something on the job. But I took it privately—if you want answers, you'll pay for them. Meantime, I'll negotiate on the gems when I see you next. LOAFALONG out." I snapped off the radio switch.

I stepped through the hatch. Don and Jan broke

their clinch momentarily. "How the hell did you know I was promoting this search, Jeff?" Don demanded through caked lips, his breath ragged. "I don't like to be caught on con-jobs."

"How else—or where else—would you have gotten the grand jury dope?" I answered, slapping his shoulder. "I wish I could have told Rick Harrison...that he didn't have to worry about his daughter as much as he'd thought. He'd have died happier."

"Then you know, Jeff," Jan demanded through clouded eyes, "that I hadn't really known about Nicky? That he—that I really thought it was the jewelry that Grissölm had killed everyone for?"

"Yeah. If you'd been playing Nicky's game, Don wouldn't have known about your father's plans. If you'd known why the VOLSTOK was sunk you wouldn't have gone home. Also, Jan, I realized by the time I'd unraveled the rest, why it was you'd lied about the time of the sinking. Why your sunburn was too light. Nicky convinced you, though you'd actually broken off with him, that Grissolm had sunk the VOLSTOK only for the jewels, that since the act was committed and Grissolm dead so you couldn't avenge it, there was no use having the boat found since the evidence aboard it—though mostly lies, he doubtless contended—was better undiscovered. Maybe he was bargaining on your divorce request, too. And I imagine you came out with them because you just couldn't stay away. You should have taken my word you'd be better off when I refused to let you come with me. For now, stop stewing. We're going to a little town on Andros Island—Andros Town. Where no one knows us or about us, where we can swim, fish, vacation, eat, and loaf...and try to forget a few things. It'll be a slow trip, we're too short-crewed to run the Owens; we'll have to tow it. And it's getting late... Start all," I called to Red. "Let's get the heck out of here."

——————

chapter

eighteen

Gia and I lay on a beach of clean pink sand. A few yards away gentle surf sloshed sibilantly against the transom of the speedboat. Cruising gulls added color and motion to an otherwise unblemished sky. We could have taken a trip back into history, might well have been the first humans to intrude into the magnificence of the tropical scene.

Like myself, Gia was burned a deep bronze after a week or more in the sea and sun; now she was an accomplished diver, skier, and still better swimmer.

Things hadn't been so calm a few days back. I grinned sardonically, remembering my comment that we'd vacation where no one knew us when we were still anchored at the reef. The newspaper men of three nations had hit Andros Town almost as fast as we did. There were police; American, British—and, because of the international ramifications, and the fact that the original murders and barratry had occurred in International Waters, we even had a representative of Interpol, the shadowy International Police Force, clearing agency for the world's criminality, headquartered in Europe.

And there were a couple of senators—from the Rackets Committee. And a Brotherhood shyster challenging my salvage claim for the Owens, since I had killed the crew. I told him I'd never seen them aboard, that it was aboard the LOAFALONG only that I'd known of them, and the vessel had not been manned within the scope of my positive knowledge. I needn't have offered him a defense, though; his name was in the testimony and the police took him away. Disbarment proceedings were started at about that time.

Between the evidence—and what some other hoodlums feared it might contain, the Brotherhood was completely depopulated at the officer-level in every seaport on the coast. They'd elect some decent Joes out of the ranks, I supposed, and run quietly for a little while.

The newspapers were ultimately sated. And the police. And the senators. Finally we settled back and took a deep collective breath, turned our vision from reports to the paradise of tropical island that surrounded us. And I'd insisted upon adding a day to our stay for every day we were bothered by the pack.

Gia rolled her head up onto my shoulder as I flexed the arm.

"I could just go on forever like this, Jeff," she murmured. "It's the most wonderful thing that's ever happened to me. Do we dive again this afternoon?"

I grinned. "I don't know whether I'll recover that soon or not."

"Anyhow," she laughed, running her fingers lightly down my ribs, "you found out it could be done."

"Yeah," I agreed, stifling a sun and sea-induced yawn, "but the next time I'll wear about two extra weight-belts!"